Totally Bound Publis

The l
Re
S

Haunted By You
I Heard Your Voice

Clandestine Classics
The Tenant of Wildfell Hall

What's her Secret?

PHOTOGRAPH

TANITH DAVENPORT

Photograph
ISBN # 978-1-78184-779-4
©Copyright Tanith Davenport 2014
Cover Art by Posh Gosh ©Copyright April 2014
Interior text design by Claire Siemaszkiewicz
Totally Bound Publishing

Published in 2014 by Totally Bound Publishing, Newland House, The Point, Weaver Road, Lincoln, LN6 3QN, United Kingdom.

Totally Bound Publishing is an imprint of Total-E-Ntwined Limited.

PHOTOGRAPH

Dedication

With thanks to Valerie Holmes, Julie Cohen and Emma Darwin for their guidance, and to Dharini, who was always happy to let me tap her medical brain.

Chapter One

The packing was finally done, and she could relax.

It was a beautiful day. As she came out of the house, Azure paused to look around, taking in the view. A protective line of trees surrounded the mansion. Before her were flower beds and lush grass, and in the distance the tips and curves of iron structures — rollercoasters in the Land of Light, the theme park attached to the property.

Sunlight peeked through the trees, dappling the lawn. Her sunglasses perched on top of her brunette head, Azure made her way across the grass, her hand automatically finding its way to her back pocket as she walked.

The familiar hard shape met her fingers. *Good.* Her mobile phone was still there.

All the preparation was finally coming to fruition. Tomorrow they would be on their way. First stop Majorca, three nights in the villa, then they would meet the Sugiyamas and their yacht — if the Sugiyamas were on schedule. Nik usually was, but Tracey could easily have made them late.

Tracey. Azure grimaced. God, this trip had better be worth it.

The planning had taken a week. She had chosen what to pack—the maids had packed it. It had all sounded so straightforward, and indeed it had been once their newest maid, Janice, had been taken off the job. She had managed to ruin three dresses by stacking them over a bottle of perfume and dumping a pair of boots on top. Azure's husband, Liam, had been decidedly unimpressed.

Right now he was back in the house checking their flight details. Azure had left as soon as she had placed the order for lunch and dinner with their cook. It was a beautiful day and the garden had been calling to her.

Ahead of her stood a white trellis bedecked with climbing pink roses. Azure followed the path through it and came out into the rose garden.

It was her favorite part of the grounds. Footpaths formed a maze through rows of multi-colored roses, leading to a fountain in the center, three mermaids spilling water from urns into a broad pool. Azure sat down on a wooden bench and leaned into the violet roses beside her, closing her eyes as the scent enveloped her.

Liam's words from that morning floated back into her head.

'It'll be fine. She said she would come.'

Tara.

A heavy sensation settled in her gut. It had been such a long time since she had seen her sister. And for such a ridiculous reason. But for Tara it had obviously been serious to have held onto it for so long.

Would she change her mind at the last minute and not come?

Show up and scream at her?

Blank her completely?

No. She wouldn't.

Tara wasn't the sort of person to waste her time. It would be pointless for her to bother coming if she had no intention of speaking to Azure. Given that Tara didn't know any of the other guests, it would make for a very lonely cruise.

An image of Tara circulating in the yacht's dining room, befriending everyone while ignoring Azure's table, came to mind. Azure shook her head, forcing herself back to reality.

It was done. There was nothing for it now but to make the trip and hope.

As a light breeze flowed through the clearing, a rustling could be heard in the bushes over the splash of the fountain. Azure's head snapped round in the direction of the sound, her hand automatically touching her back pocket again. *Was that —?*

She listened.

Silence.

Idiot. It was the wind. You know they can't get in here.

She took a deep breath and pressed a hand to her chest, feeling her heart racing. To her annoyance, her fingers were shaking.

Calm the fuck down! It was nothing!

It was ridiculous. Security was airtight around the mansion and she was miles away from any public areas. If she listened hard, she could just make out the roar of the rollercoasters and the faint screams of the riders, but nobody could get from there to here. Very few people even knew where the mansion was. It was concealed from view as much as physically possible by trees, land and fences.

Still, her body was attuned to every possible hint of danger. She had hoped to train herself out of it, but it

had been three years since her honorable discharge —
and despite the therapy, despite *everything*, she was
wound as tight as a coiled spring.

And the nightmares. Oh God, the nightmares.

You're safe here. You know you're safe here.

She did know. And she would be safe on the yacht.
No cameras following them. No crowds, no noise. It
would be fine.

She turned to go back to the house. Liam was always
able to settle her nerves. He knew what she needed —
what she wanted.

It would be fine.

As the house came back into view, she could see him
standing in the doorway, waving to her. Azure waved
back, smiling.

She would be fine.

* * * *

It wasn't going to be fine. It was going to be hell.

She had been standing in front of the bedroom
window for fifteen minutes, staring out over the
grounds, unable to drag herself away. Usually the
sight of the swaying trees, the flower beds dotted
about the lawn, calmed her. Not today. It was
physically impossible for her to relax.

Everything around her drove her crazy. The carpet
made her feet itch. The ceiling fan's gentle *whomp*
seemed twice as loud as usual. She had tried lying on
the four-poster bed and had found herself obsessively
picking threads in the curtains. Nothing could settle
her.

"You're panicking, aren't you?"

Liam's voice behind her brought her back to her
senses.

Azure turned to see her husband closing the door behind him.

Click.

"I know I'm being silly."

Liam shook his head, crossing the room toward her as he spoke, "You're not. But I think you need something to draw your attention away... Right?" On that last word he cocked his head to one side, a wicked glint in his eye.

Azure felt a slow smile kink her lips as she recognized his mood.

Something to draw her attention, indeed.

"Is this something I should be naked for, maybe?"

Liam arched an eyebrow. "I think that might help."

Holding his gaze, Azure slowly lifted the edge of her top up and over her face. She deliberately took her time, keeping her hands above her head for as long as possible, letting him absorb the view.

When she finally threw the garment on the floor, Liam had taken a step closer, the smile gone from his face to be replaced by a flush of desire.

There was something about him when he was in this mood. His blue eyes would glow, his cheekbones seeming to sharpen, his muscles taut with lust. His curly blond hair was even messier than usual—he liked to run his hands through it when he was thinking. Even though he was wearing most of a suit—shirt and trousers, no tie and for some reason, no shoes or socks—he gave the impression of an attractive, yet nutty professor.

And he was looking at her as though he wanted to ravish her.

She was barefoot—her jeans met no resistance as they fell to the floor. Azure paused in front of him, dressed in nothing but a lacy blue bra and knickers, and twirled on the spot.

"It's new. Do you like it?"

Liam's voice was low. "Oh, I like it."

The roughness in his voice made her gut clench. Azure unfastened her bra and threw it across the room where it landed on the mirror. The air in the room was cool on her skin—her nipples tightened under Liam's gaze.

"You're beautiful." The words were scarcely above a whisper, and yet they sent a thrill to Azure's heart.

Turning away from him, she hooked her fingers into the waistband of her knickers. He always liked to see her bottom—she liked to show it off. She lowered the lace underwear, bending as she did so, feeling a deep flush color her skin as her pussy was exposed to him.

God, she was wet already.

As she turned back to face him, kicking her knickers aside, the look in his eyes was almost feral. She moved to stand in front of him then dropped to her knees, before reaching up to unfasten the button on his trousers.

I love doing this. I love it.

The musky scent of him, the anticipated taste and the sense of power were going to her head. She shifted on her knees as her desire sent a jolt of pleasure to her core.

He was wearing no underwear, and his already hard cock sprang forth from blond curls as she pulled his trousers over his hips, letting them fall to the floor. She leaned forward to take him in her mouth then reconsidered, instead turning her head to press her lips to his balls.

"Fuck," she heard from above her. "Oh yes…"

She held onto his thighs, feeling them tense, and drew her tongue over the silky skin, again and again, letting the tip of his cock brush her cheek as she did. Liam groaned, sliding his fingers into her hair and clutching at her, as though he longed to pull her head elsewhere.

Oh, don't worry. I'll get there.

She buried her face in the crease of his inner thigh, inhaling the scent, and felt his cock jerk against her face, as if reminding her of its existence. Pulling back, she teasingly ran her tongue along the underside, taking a tortuous course until she tasted salty pre-cum at the tip.

Liam let out a slow, shuddering breath, and Azure allowed herself a secret smile as she leaned forward to tenderly, inch by inch, take him in her mouth.

She loved to do this, loved to hear the cries Liam made as his cock hit the back of her throat, as her lips curled round the base before drawing back, back, back to caress the head and move forward again. It was her favorite way of pleasuring him. His fingers tightened in her hair—his thighs were beginning to tremble, yet she knew he was still far from his climax—they had lots of time to enjoy, and her heart was racing in anticipation.

"Wait."

Azure looked up to see Liam pulling his shirt over his head, exposing his tanned bare chest. He stepped back out of the trousers puddled around his feet and gestured toward the bed as she stood.

"Up there. I want to taste you too."

In one swift motion he threw himself back onto the bed, legs splayed in a pose that begged to be taken. Azure climbed onto the mattress and crawled alongside him before turning to fling a leg over his head, bracing herself on all fours over him. His shaft pointed straight at her face, glistening wet.

"Oh yes," Liam whispered, then his hands clasped her hips, pulling her down onto his face.

Azure dropped her head to muffle her moans against his cock, timing each suck with the delicious drag of his tongue against her clit. His fingers were sliding inside her—one finger, then two—and softly thrusting in and out, evoking the sexual act to come— assuming that they didn't both finish this way instead, because more pre-cum was leaking into her mouth and she had no desire to stop.

"Oh God!" Liam gasped, his fingers grazing her inner spot. Azure cried out as her body clenched down on him, pleasure spiraling in her gut.

She clung to him, panting, jolting with every movement of his tongue. His cock was still in her mouth, still hard, and in that moment she knew that she needed him inside her.

Now.

She moved forward, the mattress dipping beneath her, then swiveled in place so that she was facing him, kneeling over his crotch. Reaching down to steady him, she positioned his cock and began the torturous slide downwards.

"Oh yeah," Liam moaned, clutching at the soft flesh of her hips. "Please…"

She was so wet, and he was so *hard*, and he filled her slowly, her inner walls expanding to hold him. As she rested flush against him, she paused, savoring the feeling of being so damn *full*. Liam's hand slid round her thigh and dipped, parting her lips to expose her clit, and Azure shuddered, her muscles giving an involuntary squeeze.

"That's it," he whispered. "Ride me…"

His fingers were tormenting her clit now, and Azure threw her head back, wanting to hold onto the feeling for a few moments longer. She tightened her muscles on his cock, over and over, eliciting moan after moan from him as her own pleasure began to build once more.

Oh God...

Then she raised herself up and down again, first slowly then gradually moving faster to meet Liam's thrusts.

It was breathless, passionate. Every drag of his cock inside her grazed her sweet spot—every cry, every moan sent a tingle to her core. He shifted under her then sat up, pulled her against him and thrust harder, pressing her clit against his pubic bone. Her nipples brushed against his chest as they moved, their bodies locked in union, straining for completion.

Azure dropped her head onto his shoulder, clinging to him as ecstasy uncurled within her.

This was how she liked him best, this closeness, this *cradling*—warm and tender and safe when she was most vulnerable... To be encased in his arms as his cock moved inside her, her excitement mounting with every thrust.

This was the Liam that nobody saw—not the press, not the public, nobody but her.

Liam buried his face in her neck, murmuring words she could barely hear—she caught *yes* and *God* and *fuck* and it was all too much, she was crying out in bliss and Liam gave one last, hard thrust, groaning as his climax finally hit.

They lay side by side, splayed, as the ceiling fan lazily whirred above them, swishing cool air over their heated bodies.

"You feel better now?" Liam squeezed her hand.

Azure let out a long, steady breath. "Much better."

"Any time."

"I know." Azure smiled. "I may need it a lot over the next few weeks."

"I'm sure she's just as nervous as you."

Azure paused, uncertain of her answer.

She wasn't at all sure that Tara would be as nervous as her. With Tara, she could never tell. At least, not now.

Not after such a long time, and such a cold rift between them.

Liam tugged her closer and wrapped his arm around her. Rolling over, Azure snuggled into his side, accepting the comfort.

There was nothing she could do now anyway. It was done.

All she could do was wait.

* * * *

It was always the same dream.

Dazzling sun, blinding heat, wailing chaos. The roar of explosions left and right, dust and debris flying, shouting voices and screams of pain. The heavy feeling of something hitting her leg – something metal.

A gun.

As Azure ran, the feeling dissipated, and she knew her only weapon was gone.

Nowhere to hide and the constant dread as bodies fell, the realization that the next one could be…

Helpless. The feeling of utter helplessness, of knowing that there was nothing more she could do, nothing anyone could do for her. Nothing to prevent the nameless horrors that would follow.

It was painfully clear, painfully real. Frantically searching but no rescuer, no hero – no helicopter in the sky, no vehicles to pull them out, no defense, no hope.

Falling for cover, dizzy in the unbearable heat, eyes prickling with dust and sweat. Grit under her nails, in her throat, in her hair. The voices were fading into the background, gradually falling silent, and she was alone.

Except that far ahead was a blonde figure in uniform, walking away. A familiar figure.

She could barely croak, but from somewhere inside she forced the name out, screamed it, hoarse and weak. "Come back! Help me!"

The figure looked back, fixing blue eyes on her, cold and angry.

Then turned away and left her to die.

Chapter Two

Dreams are so much clearer when the room is filled with light.

Open your eyes.

She blinked, taking in the white cool of the room, the hot Majorcan rays through the glass doorway, the sparkling blue of the pool beyond.

Drifting again.

Returning to a dream filled with excited voices, with the scream of metal on metal and the roar of the rollercoaster, the screams at the top of the loop, and the looming gates ahead. Behind them a figure standing calm amidst the chaos.

Awake. Now!

Twisting to one side with a jerk, Tara opened her eyes and raised herself on one elbow.

The hotel room was white stone, lit up in the morning sunlight. It was a basic studio room with a wardrobe, kitchenette and en-suite bathroom as well as a balcony. Above the bed an antiquated air conditioning unit hung, its door open. She had switched it off overnight, unable to sleep with its rattling wail.

It was going to be a beautiful day.

The clock showed eight thirty. Plenty of time to get down to the marina to meet the motor launch. Not enough time for brooding. The invitation stood propped up where the bedside table met the wall.

Tara was beginning to wish that she'd never agreed to come on the damned trip.

Next to the invitation stood a folded letter and a photograph. The letter she would need—Tara made a mental note not to leave it behind. The photograph was one she had debated bringing at all. It was slightly bent at the corners, a little faded, but otherwise well cared for—just battered slightly from being frequently hidden.

It was a promotional shot of a man in his late thirties, wearing an expensive-looking suit and tie. His head tilted to one side knowingly, his blue eyes seeming to look deep into hers. Tara held his gaze for a moment. *If only it were true.*

She rolled onto her back and braced her feet on the mattress, closing her eyes. She imagined that the hand she now slid along the inside of her thigh was his. A soft breath escaped her as she slipped two fingers inside her cunt, using her thumb to press and rub on her clit.

Oh, yes.

With her other hand she cupped one breast, tormenting the nipple into a stiff peak. Her motions grew faster as her fingers grew slicker, the image from the photograph clear in her head. She massaged the tender spot inside as her clit pulsed under her touch, bringing herself closer and closer to the edge.

It was him touching her, him pleasuring her. His voice in her ear whispering her name, telling her what he wanted to do to her, what she could do to him. He was laving her clit with his tongue, teasing her with his fingers, spreading her lips wide to slip his cock inside her —

Oh!

She bit her lip and stifled a moan as her body tightened, pleasure rippling through her.

Maybe now she could face the day.

* * * *

One month earlier

Tara was visiting her parents. Her arrival at the military base had been met with a hug from her mother and a handshake from her father, followed by an eye roll at her dress uniform.

"Still a bloody lieutenant." He curled his lip, eyeing her through glinting metal spectacles. "Your brother made major two months ago."

Tara rolled her eyes resignedly as she passed him in the doorway. She had heard it all before. Probably over dinner he would try again to convince her to transfer out of the Royal Engineers. He was a paratrooper himself, and no other role would satisfy him.

Her mother joined her in the living room as the warming aroma of roast chicken drifted out of the kitchen, her hands full of photographs taken in unfamiliar surroundings. Older brother Roger, dark-haired and firm-jawed, in the heat and dust of Afghanistan — younger sister Izzie, rosy and blonde, smiling from a US barracks. Tara asked the usual questions and made the usual noises before a deliberate silence fell, one that she was determined not to fill.

Sighing, Mrs Thornton got up from her chair and made for the kitchen.

"I'm making a drink. Do you want anything?"

"Please. Scotch."

Her mother paused in the kitchen doorway.

"Oh, by the way. This arrived for you."

She took a small envelope from her pocket and flicked it across the room. Tara caught it and looked at it with some bemusement. The paper was rich, heavy and embossed, putting her in mind of a wedding invitation.

"What's this?"

"I don't know—open it and find out."

Bloody woman. Untucking the already-unstuck flap, Tara held the card up to the light.

You are cordially invited to join Mr and Mrs Sugiyama…

On their yacht in the Mediterranean.

Yacht?

Who the hell did she know with a *yacht?*

"Mum? Who are Mr and Mrs Sugiyama? I've never heard of them."

"They're friends of your sister's."

And with those words, everything in Tara's head went very still.

She knew what it meant.

"Of Izzie's?"

There was a moment's uncomfortable silence from the kitchen.

"No, Tara. Of Azure's."

The invitation fell from Tara's hand.

As a cold chill spread through her heart and stomach, her eyes rested on the photograph over the fireplace, taken just over two and a half years ago. Herself, ice-blonde and pale, standing straight and tall, and her darker twin sister with an arrogant yet playful tilt to her head, her black hair falling in her eyes.

Azure.

* * * *

Now, looking at the invitation, the emotion came flooding back.

It had been two years since she had seen her.

Azure was Tara's twin, identical in some ways, the same face looking back at her with deep green eyes to Tara's cool blue, framed by blue-black hair. They had the same tip-tilted nose, the same full mouth, the same height, the same uniform, but even in a photograph Azure's fire and rebellion radiated from every pore. While Tara stood slim and straight and perfect, Azure wore the Army fatigues with the casual air of one spilling out of a scandalously-cut cocktail dress, the traditional beret of the Air Corps at a lazy slant.

Nobody who met them could ever believe that they were twins. It seemed impossible that they could look so alike in features and yet so opposite in coloring and personality. Azure had loved the reactions they got when together — she would joke wickedly about how unfair it was that they couldn't switch boyfriends on a whim. Other twins could play games with their identities — *they* were like night and day.

Azure had been discharged six months after the shot had been taken.

Tara had arrived at the family home to find Azure already resident, curled up on a sofa with a hot drink on the floor beside her. It had set the tone for much of the visit. Azure had been thinner, her limbs more tightly muscular—the result, Tara assumed, of six months of deployment. She had clearly been recovering from injuries, wincing when she'd moved, which had seemed to explain her refusal to budge from the couch for hours at a time.

But Tara had felt there was something more.

"How come you were discharged?"

Azure had raised her head and looked at her with lethargic eyes. "Don't want to talk about it."

After a week Tara's sympathy had developed raw edges. Azure had never smiled—her eyes had been dead. Her confident stride looked as though it had been straining under tripled gravity. She had taken only the vaguest interest in Tara's career, asking perfunctory questions about Tara's last tour and where she was due next, but then barely listening to the answers.

Something had been wrong, but Tara had never found out what.

Now, standing in her hotel room, the cool white cocoon that kept out the glaring heat of Majorca, Tara was conscious that she was barely hours from seeing Azure again. A lot had changed since those days.

Then she had been twenty-four. Now Tara was twenty-six. In the last two years she had neither seen, contacted nor even spoken of Azure—she had pretended they were not even related.

She had wanted it that way.

* * * *

After a quick breakfast in the hotel dining room, Tara made her way through the streets of Cala D'Or toward the marina. According to the letter she had been sent, the motor-launch would be moored exactly halfway round and would have the name of the yacht emblazoned on the side.

It was a pretty little town, obviously touristic but not obnoxiously so. The streets were lined with cafés, bars and souvenir shops. From one cocktail bar she heard the screech of a parrot, a blue and yellow macaw perched on a branch near the road. Holidaymakers passed her at a slow pace, walking casually, talking quietly, and cats and dogs sunned themselves under palm trees. It was the kind of place she could have enjoyed, and for a moment she wished that she had simply chosen to visit for a holiday rather than take up the invitation of the cruise.

She knew nobody. She couldn't possibly do this. Why had she let her mother talk her into this? And to be on the yacht for such a long time. After days of pressure, she had finally agreed to send back her acceptance—but had somehow missed the part where it was for *two damn months.*

Too late to rescind, apparently. Her mother had been clear on that point. It would be rude.

But *two months!*

For a moment she stopped in the middle of the pavement, torn. She could still turn around and leave. Just a few meters away was a taxi rank. She could get in a cab, go back to Palma Airport and get on the next plane out of there.

It suddenly seemed like a wonderful idea.

Damn it, I'm being pathetic. Why am I panicking?

No. She couldn't leave. She had chosen this, and she was sticking to it.

Forcing herself to take a deep breath, she continued her walk down the main street of Cala D'Or. The marina was signposted—it should be right ahead of her.

As soon as she rounded the corner at the bottom of the street, the vision of Cala Llonga Marina stopped her in her tracks.

It was breathtaking.

Glistening silver speedboats—some capable of sleeping up to twelve people—lined it on either side, bobbing hypnotically at their moorings. To the left, a short road extended, allowing room for several parked sports cars, before giving way to a row of fishing huts—beyond, the rocks continued out to sea. The main road curved round to the right, running alongside the water's edge past several open-fronted restaurants and some small palm trees. A cool breeze stirred her hair as she stood, whilst the sound of lapping water and the splashing of fish filled the air.

The road that edged the marina was deceptively long and the halfway point less obvious than expected, given the wide curve at the far end. At a mooring just alongside a small jetty stood a man in a dark blue uniform holding a clipboard and pen, while a pure white speedboat undulated in the rippling water below—*TENDER TO SUGIYAMA YACHT* gracing its side in tasteful gold lettering. Tara could almost smell the money from ten feet away.

With a mental deep breath, she presented herself in front of the man.

"Your name?"

"Tara Thornton."

"Ah, yes." Making a tick on his sheet, the man stepped into the boat and extended one hand with a smile. "Hop in."

Taking his hand, Tara jumped in.

The man—also apparently the maritime pilot of the tender—swiftly untied the boat, pausing only to place a sign bearing its name on the pavement for the benefit of later arrivals. He threw the rope behind him, narrowly missing Tara's head, and moved to the front of the boat to take the controls. Tara leaned back in her seat in an attempt to spot the yacht, but saw nothing save for silver and white bows, sterns on either side and a narrow strip of horizon in the center.

"How many people have arrived?"

The boat roared to a start and moved forward. Fortunately the proximity of other, extremely expensive boats forced an initial speed so slow that the pilot easily heard her question.

"About eight, including you, not including Mr and Mrs Sugiyama of course."

"Of course."

"You know how many are invited, then?"

"Yes."

A guest list, among other things, had been included with the invitation. From reading it, Tara had been given to understand that there were eight two-person berths for guests on the yacht, which allowed for fourteen invitees plus the Sugiyamas. Her stomach twisted as a nasty premonition of the driver's next question struck her.

"Ah, but did you know one of them was…" The pilot paused for dramatic effect. "Liam Wilder?"

"Yes, I had heard."

Liam Wilder. The famous Liam Wilder, dazzling in public but private in person and owner of the Land of Light chain, which included multiple theme parks in multiple countries. Yes, she had heard. It was both the reason she had agreed to come, and the reason she was regretting it every minute.

The tender passed the last of the boats as the cove widened, giving way to the open sea. As it rounded a curve in the cliff, Tara leaned forward with sudden interest — the yacht was coming into view.

It was white, designed with smooth, flowing lines, rising in a dazzling flank high above the water, and extending to perhaps two hundred meters in length, the extreme broadness of the bow slimming to a stern of half its width. The bow had clearly been designed as a suntrap — one or two unfamiliar people were already leaning over the rail. The central structure stood two storeys high and was lined with rows of windows, the large panes of glass flashing in the light. On the upper deck she could just make out the blades of a small helicopter, apparently parked on its own helipad.

At the stern hung a metal ladder beside a cut-out space intended to house the tender. While the edges of the bow met at a point, the stern gave the impression of having been chopped off some distance from the tip, leaving a blunt block much like the base of an iron. Above this a set of chunky white steps zigzagged from deck to top level, cut in the center by a strongly supported platform clearly intended for diving.

It was obvious why the tender had been necessary. This would never have been able to enter the marina.

"Beautiful, isn't she?" The pilot's voice broke into her thoughts.

"Uh…yes. She's so…big."

"Got her own ballroom, pool, everything. Give me two seconds, I'll just bring it up to the steps and you can board. You're in room one, by the way."

"Thanks." Tara paused a moment, then attempted to ask the question that had been bothering her all the way out. "Has…"

"You're sharing with Miss Palmer. She's already arrived. That's her there, leaning over the rail. With Miss Buchanan."

Ah, yes. Tara had been aware that the rooms were shared. She glanced upwards and saw two blonde women leaning over the rail above them as they approached the steps at the side of the boat. One had short hair and the other wore hers long, waving in the breeze.

A low whoop from the stern caught her attention. Three young men in shorts and T-shirts nudged each other and whistled as she looked up, their laughter becoming a cheer as Tara allowed them a smile.

"The Fetzers," the pilot commented dryly. "And Mr Martone."

Hmm. Tara ran an eye over the three figures appraisingly. None of them were especially attractive, but one was slightly better-looking than the others — blond curls, firm arms, dark tan. *Maybe some workout material there.*

"Been a busy day for arrivals," the pilot added.

Tara's gut clenched at the thought that immediately suggested itself.

"Have the Wilders arrived?" *There. I've said it.*

"Not yet, no. Hold on, I'll just tie her up." The boat slowed as it reached the steps and rocked unsteadily with the waves as the pilot wrestled with the ropes. "There you go. Grab onto the handrail."

Bracing herself against the lurching of the boat, Tara stood up, grasped the handrail and, with a short leap, made her way onto and up the steps at the side of the yacht.

"Room one!" came the pilot's voice behind her as she reached the top.

Both women turned to look at her, appraisingly, before the long-haired woman detached herself from the rail and approached her. Tara looked her up and down, wondering if this was her new roommate.

The woman was slim and lightly tanned, catlike eyes deep-set in a heart-shaped face, her eyebrows slightly raised in a faintly ironic expression. Her short capri pants, casually teamed with a green T-shirt, gave the impression that she was taller than she was — her legs were long and slender, made more so by a pair of white wedge sandals.

Having been in this situation many times, Tara drew herself up to her full height and was prepared when the woman found herself face to face with her breasts. Nobody was ever prepared for her height. However, rather than make the anticipated start of surprise, the woman merely raised her head and offered her hand to shake.

"Silk Palmer. Call me Kiki. You must be my roommate."

Tara took the offered hand, making a mental note of the name.

"Tara Thornton. Good to meet you."

"You too."

Before more could be said, there was a forceful cry of "Hey!" from the figure still leaning over the rail a few feet away. The woman exuded sunny Californian energy — cropped, highlighted blonde hair capping a darkly tanned, brightly smiling face, perfect bone structure and a modelesque figure covered by a designer bikini and sarong.

"Kiki! Aren't you going to introduce me?"

A brief flicker of irritation flashed across Kiki's face, before it was replaced by a dryly social smile. "How rude of me. Tara, this is Regan Buchanan. She's in room two."

"Oh, great."

Tara opened her mouth to continue, but Regan immediately seized back control of the floor. "Isn't the marina beautiful?"

"Oh, yes—"

"I just adore it. I've been standing here for, like, an hour just watching the waves. That boat driver is so sweet, isn't he?"

"*So* sweet." *God. It's catching.*

"You're from England? I've always wanted to go to England. This is just so exciting. I mean, I've never even been out of California till now. Kiki here likes to travel, don't you, Kiki? She's from Florida, but she's been *everywhere*."

Tara exchanged smiles with Kiki as the three of them leaned over the rail. Kiki's casual, relaxed demeanor suggested that it was far easier to allow Regan to talk herself out.

"So how do you know Tracey?"

Tracey, Tara knew, was Mrs Sugiyama, the co-owner of the yacht.

"I don't. She's friends with my sister."

"Oh? Who's your sister?"

"Azure."

Regan's jaw dropped.

"Azure? Your sister is *Azure?* Oh my God…"

But Tara was no longer listening. Her eyes were focused on another boat that was roaring out of the marina.

"I can't believe it. Oh yes, I can see it now, you do look like her! I mean, I've only ever seen her in photos or in the press, you know, but God!"

The speedboat, still distant, was bouncing over the waves, white water churning in its wake.

"Is it not weird for you? I mean, to have someone as famous as your sister—"

"She's been her sister for years," said Kiki dryly.

"Well, you know what I mean." Regan was already off on another thought. "Just—God, Azure Wilder!"

Closer. Carving through the glittering blue water, throwing up white diamonds of spray.

"And to have Liam Wilder as your brother-in-law! What did you think when you met him?"

Tara's hands gripped the rail as her gaze froze on the approaching boat. By now three figures were visible—one steering, one seated and one dark-haired figure standing at the front.

Azure.

Chapter Three

It was like being wrapped in a giant gilded leaf.

The cabin was painted in shades of green and gold, elegant yet simple, with light cotton curtains edging windows that extended across most of the exterior wall. On the side farthest from the door stood twin beds separated by polished wooden flooring, each with a small bedside table bolted to the wall. In the en-suite bathroom Kiki was blow-drying her hair, while in front of the gold-edged mirror Tara stood considering which dress to wear to dinner.

Kiki's voice made itself heard over the roar of the hairdryer. "Just pick one!"

Glancing over her shoulder, Tara caught Kiki's eye in the bathroom mirror and saw her shake her head in amusement. She turned back to the wardrobe, drew out two dresses on hangers and held them both up to the light. One was red, floor-length, made in satin with a halter neck. A long slit up the side of the left leg came to mid-thigh and the other side was decorated with a swirling pattern of sequins. The second dress was shorter and simpler, chosen after she had already thrown aside three dresses for being either too elaborate, too tight or showing too much skin.

A running commentary began from the bathroom.

"Hold out the left one. No, further. Okay, now the other one. Oh, *yes*." Her voice took on a disturbingly orgasmic quality. "*That* one, definitely. That is *heavenly*."

"Do you want me to wear it or let you sleep with it?"

Kiki chuckled. "Hang it next to mine and maybe they'll mate."

Laughing, Tara returned the red ball gown to the wardrobe and began to unhook the second dress from its hanger. It was white silk, the neckline modest, balancing the shortness of the skirt, which was slashed asymmetrically from calf to mid-thigh. Not for anyone ashamed of their legs — which, frankly, she wasn't.

She was just styling the last sections of her hair when Kiki's reflection appeared beside hers, half clad in a green one-shouldered dress that she was struggling to fasten. Tara laid down the hair straightener and made to help Kiki with the zip, noting at the same time the rather spectacular emerald choker fastened around Kiki's neck. She was wearing a diamond choker herself, but its simplicity made it invisible in the light of Kiki's dazzling green jewels.

"Nice necklace."

"Oh, thanks." Kiki turned to check her appearance in the mirror, adjusting one of the pins in her chignon. "Azure got it for me."

Tara made a noncommittal noise, deliberately leaning closer to the mirror to avoid Kiki's eyes.

"Bridesmaid gift," Kiki continued cheerfully, stepping back to view herself full-length. "Did I see you at her wedding? I don't remember."

"No. I was posted abroad."

She felt sharp eyes on her for a moment.

"I see."

"Are you ready?" Tara cut in, irritated with herself for her own curtness. It had been the truth, after all. She had been posted abroad at the time of Azure's wedding.

Admittedly she hadn't *known* she would be abroad when the response card had been put in the mail a mere day following its arrival, but that was neither here nor there.

Kiki nodded slowly and picked up her handbag, gesturing toward the cabin door. Tara followed, trying to ignore the sudden clenching in her stomach.

The cool air hit her like a wave, and she was still recovering from the change when Kiki cleared her throat.

"Are you feeling better now?"

Tara blinked, confused, then remembered. Earlier, as the tender carrying Azure had reached the yacht, she had pleaded a bout of seasickness and fled to the cabin. Regan had still been in mid-flow and had barely noticed, but Kiki had offered to help. Tara could still remember the odd look on Kiki's face when she had hastily refused, wanting to get away.

She just hadn't been ready to speak to Azure. But explaining that would have been impossible.

"Yeah, thanks. I'm fine."

Kiki nodded, apparently accepting this. "So have you actually met Liam?"

"No," Tara answered too quickly, and inwardly cursed.

"First for you then," Kiki replied.

"I guess so."

The remainder of the walk down to the dining room was spent in silence, but Tara could sense the cogs turning in Kiki's head, and Tara's stomach seemed to tighten even further.

She *had* met him. Once.

But that was different. It had been at her local Land of Light, a public meet and greet. And Liam Wilder had worn his public face the whole time.

To meet him like this was a nightmare, and she could only hope to hide it from everyone.

She had known of Liam Wilder almost all her life.

A favorite walk for the eight-year-old Tara had been a country lane near the military base. Sheltered by overhanging trees for the most part, it suddenly opened out onto a slope that led down to a sweep of tarmac — the driveway to the gates of the Land of Light theme park.

To eight-year-old eyes, it had been like the gateway to heaven. Through the red-painted bars could be seen two rows of shops shaped like chalets, sparkling with artificial snow and glittering with fairy lights. Beyond rose the mysterious metal twists of the towering rollercoasters. And ringing in her ears, the roar of wheels had mixed with the happy laughter and excited screams of the visitors.

The owner of the park was Liam Wilder.

He was known to be somewhat reclusive even on the occasions that he was in Britain. She had gathered that he spent most of his time at his largest park in California, where he had a mansion. However, he had made a number of television appearances over the years, and had appeared in several adverts for the Land of Light, all of which Tara had followed with wide-eyed admiration.

Liam Wilder.

An enigma to the world — his adverts had shown a tall, slim, soft-voiced man with a warm, friendly demeanor, his blue eyes glowing when he smiled, his light hair somewhere between blond and brown in soft curls that were mainly hidden by a straw boater.

Yet at the livelier points of his commercials, Liam Wilder would erupt with boundless energy. He could move from dreamy-eyed thought to spiraling insanity in a moment—eyes flashing, movements swift and purposeful, hat thrown aside to reveal a shock of electrified hair. He could speak with a gentle welcome or an undercurrent of excitement and danger. And Tara had worshiped him.

Worshiped him.

An eight-year-old girl's crush on a significantly older man had been easily discarded. And certainly, as she had grown, Tara had been no fool. Her crush had been pushed aside by training and teenage life. But she had still surreptitiously kept his photo in her bedside cabinet at Sandhurst, still taken pleasure in his TV appearances. He had, after all, been *her* Liam Wilder—had been for almost as long as she could remember.

* * * *

From the chandeliers hanging from the ceiling to the candelabra on each table, not a single element of the dining room décor seemed safe from dripping diamante.

A sparkling gold placeholder sat in the center of the table, emblazoned with a black number one. Orders placed, conversation with Kiki had been taken up with naming of the other guests—at least, *some* of the other guests—several were just as unknown to Kiki as they were to Tara. It had served as a salutary reminder that their hostess was Tracey Sugiyama, not Azure—her sense of being watched by a galaxy of knowing eyes was fading slowly.

Now, as the starters were placed in front of them, their small talk had hit a lull that Tara felt obliged to fill.

"So how long have you known Azure?"

Kiki took a mouthful of tomato gnocchi, chewed it for a moment and swallowed before answering.

"About two years. I work at the Land of Light in California, so I met her when she first arrived."

So she knows how they met. Ugh. Tara suppressed a wince at the memory and latched gratefully onto the earlier piece of information.

"What do you do there?"

"I'm in the finance office. Mostly I handle investors, like the Sugiyamas."

Tara nodded, automatically glancing across the room to where a Japanese couple were dining. Kiki had offered to introduce her to them during the dancing following the meal. Casually Tara let her eyes wander farther, toward an empty section at the other end of the room.

Where are they?

A bump vibrated the table, jolting Tara from her reverie. As she turned back to her tablemate, she immediately met a pair of sardonic blue eyes, narrowed as if in recognition of something unspoken. Feigning innocence, Tara picked up her fork and focused her attention on her melon starter, uncomfortably aware that Kiki's attention had not shifted.

"Are you looking forward to meeting Liam?"

Fork in mid-air, Tara paused. "Yes."

"Good. 'Cause he's just walked in."

Tara froze for a second then turned slowly in her seat, keeping her gaze steady as if she were idly scanning the room. Kiki would not be fooled—but heaven forbid anyone else in the room should think she was a star-struck idiot.

Seats around her were shifting, suggesting that the other guests had also turned in recognition—surely they would all know him, even if they didn't know Azure.

If I look at him, I'll stare...

Tara's eyes caught, cleared, and all excuses were forgotten as her gaze was sharply snagged by Azure.

The last time they had seen each other, Azure had been recovering but still downtrodden, still defeated. The figure now approaching the far tables was so far removed from this as to be almost unrecognisable. Dressed in a floor-length evening gown in deep red, a long slit in the skirt revealing a tanned leg, Azure carried herself as though she owned and deserved the worship of every person in the room. Her hair, which had previously been cut short, was now falling in a jet-black mane around her bare shoulders, cut in a blunt asymmetric fringe that revealed only one kohl-edged eye. Traveling lower, a glistening diamond necklace trailed into her cleavage, considerably more exposed than Tara had ever dared to try.

Standing next to her husband—*her husband*—Azure appeared taller than she had ever done. While Tara had always worn her height like a uniform, Azure had worn hers like a casual coat one might leave open, carefree and loose, hands thrust into the pockets. Her curves, her relaxed stance, her playful movements had all diminished her—but now, although the swell of her hips and breasts was even more pronounced than before, Azure was every inch of six feet tall, her head level with his.

Him.

It was strange to see him in a formal suit. Even stranger to see him pulling out a chair for the woman she had only two years ago called her sister. Tara's fingers gripped the back of her seat, her body tensing with restraint. The Liam Wilder of the commercials was exciting, unpredictable, unknowable. He was at once warm and passionate, calming and vital, crackling with energy to the tips of his hair — which even now was still in uncontrollable blond curls, the only point in which Tara could recognize the man from her photograph.

A wave of feeling, both dreamy and cloying, seemed to descend upon her. It was the moment she had pictured for so long, and yet, at the same time, was a resounding slap in the face. For she had been remembering Liam Wilder the character, and in front of her was Liam Wilder the man, and Liam Wilder the man was married to Azure.

Impossible, unknowable, and her brother-in-law.

* * * *

"Tracey, Nik, this is Tara."

Tara automatically thrust out her hand, wondering if her cheeks would ever settle back into their usual place. The fake smile was getting wearing.

Introductions were easy. She was used to meeting new people, remembering names, gathering pieces of information to slot them into the military hierarchy. It was something that could be done on autopilot — impatience and irritation and frayed nerves concealed behind a plastered-on smile and a shield of small talk.

Another waiter floated past with a tray of champagne flutes, one of which found its way into her hand.

Tracey was a petite, attractive woman who spoke excellent American-accented English. She was immaculately dressed and dripping with diamonds, alongside an equally short but considerably older man in an elegantly tailored suit. *Trophy wife,* sneered the voice in Tara's head, even as she smiled and murmured platitudes—"So nice to meet you", "So kind of you to invite me" – *why the hell would they invite me?* – "We must talk later…"

"Oh, there's Ryan." Kiki's voice rose. "Hey, Ryan! Ryan Hyde—he's the Sugiyamas' accountant."

Tara took the offered hand, smiling up—*up!*—at the man in front of her. Her neck seemed to give an audible sigh of relief. Tall, blond, with sharp cheekbones and a pointed jawline, Ryan was slimmer than the men she was used to and narrower across the shoulders, but had a firm handshake that called to mind a number of formidable generals.

And over his shoulder she could see…

A familiar glint had appeared in Ryan's green eyes, obviously drawing conclusions from her determined stare, but at the edges of her vision she could see a Kiki-shaped figure greeting them, ushering them forward, and it was all she could do not to—

"Hi, Tara."

It was no longer possible to ignore. Stiffening her spine, Tara turned and faced the sister she had refused to acknowledge for the past two years.

Up close, Azure's untouchable veneer had vanished—the familiarity of that half-arrogant twist to her mouth, softened by the warmth in her eyes, struck Tara like a knife to the stomach. The pull toward her was almost irresistible, and for a moment Tara forgot everything that had passed. Then, as she felt her face crease into an affectionate smile, her attention was drawn by the dark-sleeved arm stretching behind Azure's back.

Him.

It was too late for any other recourse. Tara retreated behind her cheerful mask. "Azure! Good to see you."

Inwardly she steeled herself as the friendliness fled from Azure's expression, to be replaced by a sunny smile Tara knew to be as false as her own.

"It's been a while."

"It has."

Okay. This is getting awkward.

Azure stepped slightly to one side, allowing the man beside her to move forward.

"Have you met Liam?"

So it would be this — the polite fiction of introductions. Of course, Azure had no idea they had already met. Tara bit her lip, her gut churning. *Oh God.*

His hand was already outstretched. Tara held her breath as she took it, already knowing that this would test her control far more than Azure had done. Smiling, she raised her head and allowed herself to look at him properly for the first time that evening.

Would he remember her?

"Nice to meet you, Liam," she said, and tried to sound as though she meant it.

"The pleasure's mine," Liam answered warmly. He showed no sign of recognition, and Tara's gut clenched. She had hoped for some spark in his eyes — maybe not one he could acknowledge in front of Azure, but *something* that would tell her that he remembered who she was.

And clearly he didn't. The flush that was heating her skin made her inwardly cringe.

This man was a stranger to her.

It isn't him. It isn't Liam Wilder.

Liam's voice was soft, slightly fey exactly as she remembered — the depth of feeling in his eyes matched his commercials. But there was no excitement, no suddenness to his movements, no danger — except in the strange thrill that was running over her skin at the touch of his hand. That hand should have been hers, and yet it was Azure's.

And he was wearing a suit and tie. In his commercials he had a costume — a velvet frock coat, a shirt with ruffled throat, that straw boater. To see him in a suit, just like anyone might wear, was just wrong. This was the private Liam Wilder, not the public face she had only ever seen.

It wasn't right. It just wasn't *right*.

And if Azure had told him...

It was impossible to relax as Liam talked, impossible to focus on her unnaturally slick responses to his polite questions. The Liam of her mind spoke to her alone, but this Liam was speaking to his wife's sister, and her façade was growing brittle, every inch of her screaming for someone to step in and rescue her from the conversation.

By the time Kiki excused them both, pleading an urge to try out the vodka-shot bar, Tara was ready to run screaming from the room, and the row of fruit-flavored shots Kiki lined up in front of her was almost all empty before she could forget Liam's hand in hers or the strange expression on her sister's face.

* * * *

Eleven p.m. and Tara was quite cataclysmically drunk.

Introductions finally complete, she had found herself seated at a corner table with a small group of other singles — Kiki, Regan and a broad-shouldered girl with cropped dark hair, roommate and client of Regan's marketing firm. Confiding in Tara her hopes of being hired by the Land of Light as a DJ, she had hinted heavily at Tara's ability to drop words into Liam Wilder's ear. Fortunately, though, as the alcohol had flowed, the hints had ceased, replaced by rambling. She was now lying in a giggling heap along a banquette seat, occasionally mumbling something unintelligible to Regan, who had been drinking mocktails most of the evening and was chatting away to someone on her mobile phone.

Tara stood up from the table, still holding her half-full cocktail glass. Beside her Kiki, who was slumped in her seat, made an incoherent noise of surprise.

"'M off to get some air."

Kiki's mouth moved, but her eyes remained fixed on empty space. "'Kay."

The room swayed queasily as Tara made her unsteady way across the almost deserted dance floor toward the staircase, glass held out ahead of her like a flaming torch.

A figure stepped out in front of her, and she gasped.

"Sorry. I didn't mean to startle you."

Tara focused uncertainly on the face in front of her. Blond curls, deep-set blue eyes in a lightly tanned, oval face gradually formed themselves. The memory rose of a catcalling figure in sunlight, and Tara smiled as she finally recognized him.

He was the cute guy she'd seen at the rail.

Up close he was probably better-looking, although considerably younger than she had thought at first glance—nevertheless, he would do for one night.

But not tonight. She was far too drunk.

"Hi. I'm Tara."

"Good to meet you, Tara." His voice was higher than she had expected, lightly flavored with an American accent. "I'm Reese. Reese Fetzer."

"Hi, Reese." Tara deliberately lowered her voice, adding a breathy touch, and was gratified to see Reese's eyes brighten with interest.

"I saw you arrive, didn't I? You're sharing a room with Kiki?"

"You know Kiki?" Okay, so obviously he did, but the little tilt to her head and wide-eyed stare worked better on men when combined with a certain amount of sweet stupidity.

"We've met at parties," Reese responded with a smile that broadened as Tara leaned forward, allowing him a flash of cleavage.

"Who are you sharing with?"

"My brother Mal. He's over there."

Tara turned as Reese pointed, but didn't bother to really look. Instead she deliberately stumbled forward a little, forcing him to catch her arms and steady her.

"Whoa there! Think someone's had a little too much."

"Mmm." Tara lifted her eyes to his. "I think I need to lie down."

She paused just long enough for Reese's eyes to widen as he caught her meaning—or what he thought was her meaning.

"Guess I'll see you tomorrow," she breathed, and slid away through the door before he could answer.

It was cooler already in the stairwell, the night air seeping in through the exterior door, but Tara was still unprepared for the sudden cold slap as she stepped out onto the deserted deck, lurching forward and turning to lean back on the rail.

Out here the stillness of the night was overwhelming—an eerie silence broken only by the gentle splash of waves against the sides of the yacht. The deck was softly lit, and Tara let her head fall back, her vision filling with the velvety dark sky and pinpricks of stars, spiraling slowly, edged with a dreamy golden glow.

Another figure floated out onto the deck, drifting to a stop beside her, and Tara was pulled from her reverie to see Azure, bathed in moonlight and lamplight, her black hair a softly-ruffling cloud framing heavy eyelids and a lopsided smile. Even now Tara remembered that face, the one Azure wore when she came in late at night, and found herself unable to resist smiling back.

"You're drunk," she said, hearing her own voice slurring slightly.

"So are you," Azure threw back intelligently. "What're you drinking?"

"Pina colada. You?"

Azure took a sip from her own glass and winced. "Vodka martini. Tastes like the barman stirred it with his foreskin."

An inelegant snort escaped Tara before she could contain it. God, she had almost forgotten her sister's filthy mouth. Instinctually she bumped Azure with her shoulder, laughing as Azure promptly retaliated with more force and knocked her off balance. The motion of the boat caught her unawares as she straightened up and fell back against the railing with a startled gasp.

"Shit." Azure set her drink down on the floor and put an arm around her. "Are you okay?"

Tara looked up, opening her mouth to reassure her sister, and was suddenly struck by a memory of the last time they had stood like this.

The day Azure had left.

"You're nuts. You know nothing's going to happen."

"I know."

Only it had. Azure had left, and one morning Tara had picked up the newspaper to see —

"I'm fine," she said coldly, sidling out of Azure's embrace. "I'm going inside."

Azure's arms dropped to her sides.

Moving away from the side of the boat, Tara steeled herself for an angry retort. Azure had never been one to accept rejection silently.

Nothing.

Azure was standing with arms folded, staring at her fiercely, but with her mouth set in a firm line as if she were struggling for control. Tara waited for a moment, watching for her to snap.

Go on. Just do it.

Shaking her head, Azure looked away, letting out her breath in one frustrated rush. Tara turned to make her way back to the stairs.

"You're a fucking idiot," Azure said to her back.

Tara's shoulders stiffened.

"And you're a whore."

The door to the stairs was heavy, but made a very satisfying slam.

Chapter Four

Bathed in a combination of screen glow and filtered morning sunlight, Azure leaned back in the leather chair and stared absently at the computer. Behind her the bathroom door hung half open, sounds of movement audible over the roar of the shower.

Tracey had told her that the daily menus would be available on the onboard intranet, and so they were. Listed onscreen were the options for lunch and dinner — *jellied consommé, scallops, herb-encrusted lamb* — item after item, many of which were either her or Liam's favorites. Azure's eyebrow arched sardonically. God, what a display of boot-licking this was turning out to be.

The writing desk was almost identical to her own at home, the mahogany looking distinctly incongruous next to the PC. Azure had filled the shelves with photographs, books and keepsakes — a large jewelry box stood open at the far end, a gold bracelet spilling out onto the wood. Above the monitor stood her wedding photograph, alongside a larger frame that held a number of smaller family shots. It had been impossible to find one photo with everyone in it. Nobody in the Thornton family stayed in the same place at the same time.

The blonde, poised image of her twin seemed to jeer at her from the frame.

Damn Tara.

She had known that afternoon two years ago that Tara would take it hard.

The wedding invitations had been spread all over Liam's writing desk—now her own. She had paused over her twin's as though approaching a landmine. It would have been a stab, even when expected.

If only the bloody press hadn't gotten there first.

She'd been warned that everything Liam did was in the news within a few days, but this had been fast even for them. Liam had shown her the headlines, his face flushed with anger.

"We're already trending. Looks like we've got another informer in the company."

"Shit." Azure had called the house immediately, but it had already been too late.

"What's happening?" Her mother's voice had been almost a shriek. "Why are the papers saying you're getting married?"

"Mum, I'm really sorry. I meant to tell you first."

"Never mind that! You've been there a *week!* How can you possibly know him well enough to marry him?"

It had been a difficult question to answer. Azure had known that a week was brief even in terms of whirlwind romances. The newspapers had had a field day with their speculations about the timeline, even wondering if they had been secretly dating beforehand. PR statements had already been being prepared, but even with those and the interviews

Azure had heard were being scheduled, she had known it would be impossible to completely quell the gossip, simply because it was such an unusual occurrence. From meeting to engagement in one week? It was beyond most people's ability to grasp.

Even hers, in fact.

She had never been a person to leap into relationships. For one thing, life in the military had created problems — she hated dating long distance. For another, her father had loathed every man she had ever introduced to him. It was easier just to avoid the issue wherever possible.

But when she had returned from her deployment, honourably discharged owing to injury, somehow nothing else had seemed to matter. Her mother's worry, her father's stiff upper lip, her sister's utter lack of understanding had all seemed to pass by in a haze. When she had met Liam and found herself falling, the overwhelming thought in her mind had been simple — *What the hell?*

Nobody's opinions mattered anymore but her own, and if people thought she was crazy, well... Let them think that. She was happy. Liam was happy. Things went wrong in marriages all the time, even those between people who had known each other for years. Why shouldn't theirs work out? What did she have to lose?

Of course, she hadn't wanted to alienate her family. Settling the details, clearing truth from fiction, had taken time, but her mother was ultimately mollified and her father was almost proud. He chose to ignore it, but she knew he had guessed how much she disliked her career. If he could take pride in her marriage, in being able to say *my daughter, Azure Wilder,* then that was good enough for her. And once her mother had overcome her reservations about the speed of their courtship and the twenty year age gap, she had been ready to hear about the wedding arrangements and bask in the glory of her daughter getting married. She had even insisted on flying out to help with the planning.

But Tara…

"Is Tara there?" she had asked, hoping against hope.

Her mother had paused. "She's not in at the moment." Her voice had been uncomfortable, and Azure had chosen not to push it. She had thought that maybe Tara had just needed time.

But Tara had remained 'out' through call after call, at all hours of the day or night. The invitation had been Azure's last attempt at making contact, writing her home number by hand on the card in the hope of a personal reply.

When the impersonal response card had returned in the mail, Azure had known that there was no chance. The trumpet cry of that damned headline had deafened Tara to any plea for rationality.

Then last night…

Fuck it.

The shower snapped off, and after a few moments Liam padded through the doorway, a mint-green towel wrapped round his waist and another hanging from his neck. Azure swung round in the chair to face him, automatically switching the monitor off at the same time.

"I laid out your red stripe, if that's okay."

"Oh, that's fine." Liam glanced over to the bed, where a faintly striped shirt lay above a pair of black jeans, before starting to towel his hair. His next words were muffled, the only audible words being "night" and "screaming".

"Pardon?"

"I said" — Liam draped the towel over the top of the wardrobe door — "did you sleep okay last night? You were screaming again."

"Oh." Azure shifted uncomfortably. "Yeah. Yeah, I did, it was fine. Sorry."

"Don't be sorry." Liam was buttoning the shirt, his lower half still covered by the second towel. "It was only once, and you know how I sleep."

"Like a rock," said Azure, treating him to a smile. She glanced at her watch. Eight thirty a.m.

"Breakfast," Liam said, echoing her thought. "And then you said, didn't you, you wanted to — "

"If we could, yeah."

"Sure. Breakfast and then the chapel."

"Breakfast and then the chapel," Azure agreed, standing to slip her feet into her shoes.

The faint hope of meeting Tara in the dining room flickered in her mind, before collapsing under the weight of reality. Tara had probably been up for hours.

And she'd never approach me with Liam there anyway.

* * * *

Ten a.m. and the punchbag juddered on its hook as Tara landed another roundhouse kick.

She had woken at six thirty to find the room as empty as it had been when she had fallen asleep. Kiki had never returned to the room, it appeared. Nursing a slight hangover, Tara had swallowed two Alka-Seltzers and made her way to the dining room, which had been mostly empty at that time of the morning, apart from a couple in their thirties whose names had been washed away by alcohol.

It had been a pleasant surprise to find waitress service at breakfast. Obviously such a small entourage allowed for personal attention rather than large metal trays under heat lamps. Feeling renewed after one bowl of porridge and another of stewed fruit, Tara had decided to find the on-board gym and make up for missing her workout the previous day.

Attacking the punchbag was wonderfully cathartic.

Slam.

Azure waltzing around all night with…*him.*

Kick.

Liam Wilder acting so…so un-Liam Wilder.

Punch.

Too much to think about when she had a pounding headache.

Slam.

"Well hey, Golden Girl," drawled someone with an American-accented voice behind her. "What did that punchbag ever do to you?"

Tara paused mid-punch then turned slowly, swallowing her automatically poisonous response. *Well, it called me Golden Girl, actually…*

The smirking owner of the voice was standing in the open doorway to the weights room, leaning casually on the door frame, hands thrust into the pockets of his tracksuit pants. A dark vee of sweat was outlined on his white T-shirt, and his tanned face bore that post-workout glow that Tara knew so well. The image of a black tuxedo, towering height and green eyes immediately flashed to mind.

This was the Sugiyamas' accountant.

"Ryan, isn't it? The number-cruncher." *Golden Girl, indeed.*

If Ryan was at all offended, his smile was unaffected. Pushing himself off the door frame, he crossed the room and held out one hand to shake.

"You remembered." A brief flicker of satisfaction crossed his face as Tara was forced to look up at him. "Ryan Hyde. And you're our military expert, right? Which corps?"

Tara allowed him a slightly warmer smile for his choice of epithet.

"Royal Engineers."

"Same as Azure?"

"No. Azure was Air Corps."

"And then she quit to get married." Ryan was still holding her hand, his eyes watching for any reaction. "So if you got m—"

"No, I wouldn't." Tara had heard this question many, many times before and had her response honed to perfection. "It's not hard to balance the two." She took advantage of Ryan's moment of surprise to retrieve her hand, suppressing the urge to wipe it on her shirt. Suddenly the conversation seemed very tiring.

Whether her feelings had shown in her face or the abundance of sweat had suddenly dawned on him, Ryan seemed to share her need to call a halt.

"I'm glad to hear it. And on that note, I'm going to take a shower. Maybe I'll see you later." He was already moving away, pausing only to pick up a bag inside the weights room doorway before glancing back at her as if expecting a friendly goodbye.

Relieved at her reprieve, Tara found herself smiling far more brightly than she had intended. Immediately she saw that look in his eyes again, that spark from last night when he had thought that she was staring at him.

When she had been trying not to look at...*him*.

Turning back to face her on his way into the male shower room, Ryan paused to ask, "Do you plan to work out every day?"

"Yup," Tara answered casually. "Always do."

His eyes glinted. "Looking forward to it."

Then the door banged shut behind him, leaving Tara to grab her bag and go for the fastest shower of her life.

* * * *

Finding herself in a widening hallway, the walls decorated in gold and cream, Tara came to a halt and looked around for one of the mounted wall maps. She had definitely taken a wrong turn somewhere.

In her haste to get out of the gym without encountering Ryan again, she had completely lost her sense of direction. At this point she should have been standing next to a Coke machine outside a solarium. Instead she was faced with a carved wooden door, slightly ajar, which led into a room decorated in warm reds and golds. One glance into the room, with its heavy silence and evenly spaced wooden pews, and Tara knew what it was.

It was a chapel.

The stillness of the room seemed to envelop her as she stood. Tara had never been especially religious, but worship was worthy of respect, and she found herself pausing in the doorway, resting her head on the frame.

Her eyes fell on a familiar figure at the far end of the room kneeling, dark hair falling over her lowered face, hands clasped in front of her.

Azure.

It was an unexpected sight. Azure, as Tara remembered her, had been mostly agnostic. They had attended their local church as children, but as an adult, churches had become places for weddings, christenings and funerals only. Voluntary attendance? Out of the question.

Tara wondered, uncomfortably, how many other things had changed about Azure.

The calming atmosphere was fading, replaced by an awkward sense of intrusion. Moving slowly, Tara pushed herself away from the door frame and turned to leave.

Fuck!

Liam Wilder was leaning against the opposite wall. A dispassionate corner of her roiling brain observed that this, at least, tallied with his commercials — apparently he really did have the ability to appear out of nowhere.

It took a moment for Tara to regain her composure, but if Liam noticed, he made no comment. Maybe he simply thought he had startled her. God forbid he should think of her as a screaming groupie.

You are a screaming groupie, her inner voice jeered.

Liam nodded toward the chapel door, and Tara fought to keep her heart in her chest.

"I thought I'd give her some time alone," he said softly.

"Of course," Tara murmured, hoping she sounded suitably knowledgeable about her sister's habits. Maybe he thought that Azure had always been spiritual.

Or maybe he was perfectly aware that she knew almost nothing about Azure anymore.

After a pause, Liam's eyes slid from the door to Tara's face.

"I'm glad you decided to come."

Tara managed to compress all her emotions into faintly surprised eyebrows.

"I know," Liam continued, still in that soft voice, "that you haven't spoken in a while…"

Oh God, oh God, oh God, what does he know? No, she can't have told him – But what if she did? Does he know how I feel? Oh God…

Clamping down on her panic, Tara nodded stiffly and tried to look impassive.

"But I'm looking forward to getting to know you."

It was ridiculous, Tara told herself. Of course he didn't mean it like that. But her heart was leaping, and she could feel her breath stuttering as she opened her mouth to answer, even as she struggled to keep her mask in place.

"Me too." *Oh, yes, me too –*

Behind her there was a slight rustle that echoed against the walls of the chapel. Liam immediately straightened, apparently attuned to every movement *she* made. Tara automatically stepped aside as he moved toward the door, averting her eyes but still conscious of his proximity as he paused just alongside her.

Oh God, he was *right there* – Liam Wilder was standing *right there* and close enough that she could feel the heat of his body, making her skin prickle, the hairs on her arms rising on end. All the time she had spent longing to see him again, to have him so close to her…

She bit her lip, her breath quickening, and *hell*, she knew she was blushing but just the memory of his last words were –

His voice, that light, musical voice, murmured close to her ear, "She really wanted you here."

Tara darted a quick glance at him behind the veil of her hair. Liam's gaze was firmly fixed on some distant object, his expression unspeakably tender as he spoke again.

"And, of course, anything that makes Azure happy is important to me."

His face crinkled into that warm smile that had always made Tara's heart swell, but now her mouth twisted into a sickening grimace, because his eyes were on Azure.

It was pathetic, utterly pathetic to feel like this — to feel bypassed by *her* Liam Wilder. Her mask slammed down, hard, her fingernails digging into her palms, jaw clenching, because she could already see how this was going to go. Longing to be seen, snapping up every scrap of notice like some over-enthusiastic lapdog, and the inevitable always-fresh stab of remembering that he was *not* her Liam Wilder but Azure's husband.

He didn't even remember having met her. She remembered everything, and for him it had been nothing. She was *nothing.*

Another rustle in the room, the sound of someone standing, and Liam immediately slipped past her into the chapel, obviously feeling that alone time was over.

To wait any longer would be just too humiliating. There was a map on the wall ahead, and Tara marched, turning her back on them both.

I hate you. Fucking bastard. I hate you, I hate you, I hate you —

As she rounded a corner, Tara's angry inner monologue was interrupted as she collided forcefully with someone coming the other way.

It was Reese.

And he was *drunk.*

"Well, hello." Slurring his words, reeking of beer, Reese clumsily gripped both her arms as he staggered, almost pulling her off her feet. "In a hurry?"

Tara stilled for a moment, forcing her irritation down as she took in the sight in front of her. God, it was pathetic. Not even midday and this idiot was paralytic. Sure, he was cute, but *ugh*, was this all there was to him?

Of course, for some purposes, that was all she needed.

"You know," Reese continued, releasing one of her arms so he could brandish his finger in her face, "you need to *slooooow dooooown*."

"Oh, but I never move slow." Tara dropped her chin to treat him to a doe-eyed look. "Too much energy, they tell me."

"Oh yeah?" A leer. "Well, if you need any help burning off that energy…"

God. I should just buy a vibrator. It would save all this shit.

But Tara had done this before, and already knew what she would do. She was pissed off, frustrated. Sex would help to ease that frustration. And she had never met a man who didn't like a no-strings fuck.

Especially not one who was smashed this early in the day.

"How about right now?"

* * * *

The door slammed. Her T-shirt, vest, jeans hit the floor. Reese's tanned body fell heavily on the mattress, bouncing slightly as Tara landed on hands and knees over him. He was wearing khaki shorts that unbuttoned easily, and nothing beneath.

Tara unsnapped her bra and, with an impatient jerk, threw it aside. Reese's eyes widened almost impossibly as, a few seconds later, her knickers flew to land on top of the mirror.

"Whoa— You're—"

Before he could say anything else, Tara bent down to kiss him, rocking her pelvis back at the same time to brush against his hardness. Reese groaned, lifting his hands to encircle her waist before sliding them higher to cup her breasts.

Faster.

Tara crawled forward along his body until she could rest her hands on the headboard, her thighs on each side of his head. Catching one brief glimpse of Reese's expression of glazed heaven, she lowered herself onto his face. Immediately his hands jerked to her hips, clenching on her buttocks as his tongue invaded her cunt.

"That's it," she whispered breathlessly, and heard him moan in response. "Right there."

Oh, it was good—he really knew what he was doing, and every time he groaned she could feel the vibration and it was— *Oh God!* Tara threw her head back, pressed down harder, felt his fingers dig in deeper and his body suddenly jolted under her—he had to be getting desperate, he was already thrusting even though…

She pulled away and shuffled backwards until the tip of his dick touched her, then in one swift movement she dropped down onto him, gasping as he filled her to the hilt.

"Fuck," Reese cried out as she arched her back and circled her hips. "Oh *fuck* —"

And their bodies were crashing together, and Tara closed her eyes as she felt her pleasure start to build, spiraling, tensing. Reese was moaning, "Oh fuck, oh fuck" as his hips rocked under her and Tara shifted her pelvis — yes, *that* was the angle she needed, and *oh, now, now...*

"Yes!"

Her body tightened as her cry echoed through the room, joined seconds later by Reese's shout of pleasure as he stiffened and collapsed beneath her.

He had still been staring wide-eyed and speechless at the ceiling ten minutes later when Tara had closed his bedroom door behind her as she left.

Chapter Five

Morning sunlight bathed the deck in blazing light, and Tara's arms prickled under heat and buttery suncream, the back of her neck already slick with moisture.

It was going to be a beautiful day to go ashore.

Beside her, leaning over the rail, Kiki was trailing her scarf in the breeze, idly watching the fabric flutter. Tara cast an unconvinced eye over her. *She's no more relaxed this morning than she was last night.*

And, oh boy, had Kiki been painful company last night.

She had genuinely thought Kiki was going to drive her insane.

It had been a mixed day. After leaving Reese's bedroom, Tara had made a full tour of the yacht, uncovering several areas that she intended to visit again — in particular the one-screen movie theater on the bottom level and the 'beauty salon', a small yet elegant room just below the guest corridors. For the first time in her life, she had the freedom to have a facial or massage whenever she chose.

She had to admit, from a physical point of view, there was really nothing to complain about. Everything about the yacht was the height of luxury. She could do what she wanted, whenever she wanted.

But, she had thought as she'd sat in her cabin, watching her roommate ponder the merits of three different pairs of shoes, *it would be much better if Kiki would hurry the hell up.*

It had been excruciating, more so because it had proven impossible to get a sensible word out of her. Where had she been last night? *'Oh, I crashed out.'* What had she done today? *'Oh, not much.'* Why not put on that pair? *'Oh, I'm not sure.'*

"I can tell you're an officer," Kiki had said, lifting her head briefly to fix Tara with a sardonic stare. "You're just dying to order me to get my ass in gear and march."

Tara had concealed her impatience behind a smile, wondering if it were really that obvious or if Kiki was psychic.

"I'd love to see you march in those shoes. You'd break your neck."

Kiki's eyes had glinted in challenge, exquisite silver six-inch heels at the ready.

Ten minutes later they had been sat at their table, Kiki with her hair hanging half out of its French twist on one side. From the expression on Regan's face as she'd taken her place at the next table, it hadn't gone unnoticed.

"Oh my God, Kiki, what happened? You look terrible! Well, I didn't mean it like *that,* but you know —"

Kiki had twisted in her seat and fixed Regan with a heavy glower. "I fell down the stairs."

Tara had bitten her lip to hide the smile that had been threatening to burst free.

"And you can shut up as well."

"Never said a word," Tara had sworn, lifting the menu to cover her face.

By the time the food had arrived, Kiki's dark annoyance had been replaced by that same air of breezy restlessness. Now, however, she seemed to find the silence unbearable. Tara had focused on her meal and weathered the initial torrent of words—*food overcooked, when do we dock again? Feet killing me*—and had fought against the urge to throw on an alcohol force-field.

Quiet would have been restful. Babbling lunacy had built annoyance like a static charge. It could only have been a matter of time before the mood had broken, and the appearance of a vision in silver-gray, capped with the choppy black bob and glitzy-bright grin of Tracey Sugiyama, had been enough to send a crackle through the heavy air.

"Good evening, ladies! Tara, darling, I do hope the food was to your liking. Stuffed peppers are your favorites, aren't they?"

Tara had allowed herself an inward moment of surprise even as her face had glazed over with an empty smile. *How does she know that?*

Of course, Azure could have told her.

But why would she make such an effort?

Oh, stop it. You're thinking too much.

Mentally shaking her head, she had glanced across at Kiki, who had been leaning back in her seat, her mouth open in a smile that had bared her teeth. Tracey had turned to face her, her head tilted softly to one side, expression beatific.

"And you, Kiki. I see you couldn't finish it. I hope the spinach wasn't a problem for you." If anything, her smile had grown sweeter.

"Oh, no," Kiki had responded, punctuating the phrase with a flicker of eyebrows. "I've grown to like it, in fact."

"Well, of course." Tracey had nodded her head understandingly. "You must have eaten a lot of vegetables on that diet."

Tara had blinked, but Kiki had remained unflinching.

"It's obviously working wonders," Tracey had continued as the wall had remained uncracked. "I mean, you must have lost at least *sixty* pou —"

Kiki's eyes had flashed.

"Oh yes. It's especially good at smoothing fat from the stomach." Teeth, glinting. "You should try it."

Unstoppably Tara's eye had been drawn to the uneven bulge at Tracey's waist. Tracey's hand had sharply moved, blocking her view, then Tracey had abruptly turned to address her.

"Well!" Her voice had been high, bitten. "We dock tomorrow morning at Tossa de Mar, so if you could be on the deck by ten —"

"Of course," Tara had cut in. There had been an itinerary in her room. She had vowed to read it as soon as she got back.

"Good. I'll see you then." A swish of fabric, and the last image Tara'd had was of a cold, pokerish back.

Okay. That was awkward. Turning back to her tablemate, Tara had opened her mouth to ask —

And had paused.

Kiki had been watching the retreat, tense-mouthed, a strange flush staining her face.

Looking at her now, the question still jumped on Tara's tongue, but Kiki's eyes were flecked with a dangerous light, and Tara had learned to value her skin. Better to begin with something less incendiary.

"Anything wrong?" she ventured carefully.

And the light extinguished.

"Nothing," Kiki muttered, turning away. "Nothing's wrong."

The morning sun highlighted her profile, and Kiki's jaw jutted.

More firmly, "Nothing's wrong."

And there was nothing to do but accept it.

* * * *

"You know," Azure said, turning from where she had been looking out of the window, "you look really quite sexy in a polo shirt."

"Why, thank you," was Liam's response. He was standing in front of the mirror in their cabin, adjusting his collar.

Azure allowed her eyes to wander over the lines of his body, focusing on the curve of his bottom under his tan trousers. Liam always made an effort to be immaculately dressed when they were in public.

Even when no one had been told where they were.

Is he sure no one knows where we are?

It was a question Azure always left unasked. Liam hated any publicity he couldn't control. If he were willing to go ashore, he had to be confident that they would have privacy.

And yet the thought of cameras, of close-moving bodies, of fighting and slamming and the barrage of noise, refused to leave her mind and made something inside tighten.

She forced the thought out of her mind, focusing instead on her husband. He checked his hair, casually shifting his weight from foot to foot—almost as if he were trying to keep his arse in continual motion for her entertainment.

Which he probably was.

"You know," Liam continued, leaning forward in a casual movement that kept Azure's eyes fixed on his rear, "some might say it was rude to undress me with your eyes."

"Oh, shut up, you," Azure fired back, laughing. "I think I'm allowed."

Liam tilted his head as if tipping an imaginary hat. "Mmm...I *guess* you're allowed."

I bet Tara undresses him with her eyes.

Hmm. Now there was a thought worth keeping to herself.

"What are you thinking about?" came from the other side of the room.

Azure swiftly censored the twist her mouth had taken on.

"Just Tara."

"Oh, Tara." A slight arch of the eyebrow was all the surprise Liam showed, but it was enough. "How did you get there? Does *she* undress people—?"

"I doubt it," Azure cut in. *Christ, I'm not going down that route.* "Their clothes don't stay on long enough."

This time Liam's eyes widened with interest. Azure shot him a mock-warning look—he held up his hands in teasing surrender.

"Do tell."

"Not much to tell. She was always deployed. When she came home, she went out and shagged. I've not known her to have a steady boyfriend since she was seventeen."

Azure gave a loose shrug, shaking out the tension that had clenched her muscles at the reminder that in the last two years, she hadn't known Tara at all.

If Liam noticed, he had the sense not to comment beyond, "We'll have to find her someone."

"There's enough men on board," was Azure's reply. "She'll eat them alive."

A silence fell between them. Liam gave his reflection a last once-over before stepping away to stand behind Azure, smoothing away imaginary wrinkles in her jacket, the press of his hands firmer than was necessary. Azure shivered involuntarily.

"You're nervous," Liam murmured into the back of her neck.

"I know." Azure felt her teeth clench.

"Don't be."

An image of flashing bulbs and freeze-framed panic flitted across her mind, swiftly followed by an image of a cold, unresponsive Tara—one glance cast before turning her back.

I'm not sure that's possible.

* * * *

"Ten minutes, everyone. Ten minutes."

The cry from below was accompanied by creaking and bumping as the tender was untied. People clustered along the length of the port side rail. Tara glanced at them, searching, then looked away uncomfortably.

No sign of Liam and Azure.

Where were they?

God, this was pathetic. It was ridiculous to let them make her this nervous, and yet whenever she looked away she felt her spine prickle with dread.

She turned back to face the sea. A rock promontory loomed into view, bleached by sunlight, capped with the ruins of a medieval castle.

"I'll have to look round that," she commented, her hand tightening automatically on the rail as the yacht plunged over a wave.

"Muh," was Kiki's answer. It was followed by a grunt as another wave rocked the deck, sending her into an ungainly stagger.

Still watching the coastline, Tara caught Kiki's shoulder with her free hand and redirected her toward the safety of the rail.

Honestly. No sense of balance.

They were rounding the cliff now, the rocks gradually giving way to a white strip of sand. At this distance it was impossible to make out details, but the buildings along its edge were blurring into a curious mix of the traditional and the touristic — beach cafés beside more conservative restaurants, souvenir shops beside original houses.

Tara would have leaned forward to see more, but her view was abruptly blocked by a green T-shirt.

"Well, well, well," crooned a familiar, irritating voice. "If it isn't Golden Girl."

"Ah, Ryan." Tara felt her voice already taking on a taunting drawl. "I didn't think accountants came out in the sunlight."

Unaffected, Ryan smirked down at her, making full use of his three extra inches of height.

"*American* accountants do. We even surf in our spare time." He waved a hand at the panorama behind him. "So what do you think?"

"Tossa?" Tara asked innocently, taking pride in the knowledge that few Americans would grasp her dual meaning. "Gorgeous."

Ryan's smile broadened as if her second comment had been directed at him. Tara smiled back, privately grinding her teeth.

"I'm glad you think so. They're firing up the boat now, if you're ready. I'll give you a hand in."

"Thank you," said Tara as another wave sent Kiki reeling, "but I'm quite capable." Catching Kiki, she propelled her into Ryan's arms. "Give Kiki a hand in."

Ryan opened his mouth, but his response was cut off by another yell from the driver.

"All aboard! First eight!"

A quick scan of the deck showed that there was still no sign of Liam and Azure. Or Reese, thank God. Tara was first to the steps, climbing down cautiously to the tender as it bucked and reared at the end of its rope. Kiki was behind her, followed closely by Ryan and a red-haired, spindly-armed man whose name she couldn't remember. As she settled herself into the boat, Tara glanced up at the rail and saw Regan and another girl preparing to descend.

Two more.

Tracey Sugiyama and her husband were in sight, ushering others forward. One woman reached the steps, looked down at the boat, panicked.

"Oh no, no, no. I can't. I'll fall in." She stepped back, one hand over her mouth. "No, please. Someone else go ahead."

There was some debate among the others. The woman's fear rippled along the rail as eyes turned, two by two, to consider the boat as it pitched and rolled. Glancing at Kiki, Tara saw that she was already starting to look green.

"Ah, there you are," Tracey said, and her heart sank as two familiar figures appeared at the top of the steps.

Great. Them.

There was no escape to be had now. Tara busied herself with solicitously fussing over Kiki, who pleaded perfect health before hanging her head over the side and panting. Ryan was in his gallant element, patting her on the back and offering to hold her hair, a suggestion that Tara was forced to give him credit for. She was happy to assist, but when it came to helping people vomit she would have to put her foot down.

There was a slight shudder as two more bodies stepped into the tender and settled, then there was a snap of rope and the engine roared to life. Another wave rocked the boat as they began to move forward.

Thank God it would only be a brief trip.

The shoreline swam into view, blue and white and gold shimmering in the heat-haze. Tara kept her face turned toward Kiki, her hair whipping in the wind, providing a convenient barrier between her and more unsettling possibilities. Behind her voices drifted on the air, Azure's rising to the surface like cream.

"It looks beautiful, doesn't it? That castle is stunning. I should have looked this place up, I've no idea how old it is. Do you?"

Her voice was low, breathy, carrying a timbre that gave Tara pause. Under a carefree mask, she sounded...*nervous.*

Why would she be nervous?

"It's all right, Keeks," came Ryan's cheerful drawl, snatching back her attention. "We're nearly there."

Tara looked up and saw that it was true—they were approaching the promontory. A small platform jutted out from the cliff face, steps above cut into the rock. The driver turned the boat, preparing to back toward the platform.

Above her, she could hear the movement and voices of tourists.

I wonder if they'll recognize Liam?

The thought gave her a childish tang of pleasure — *I know Liam Wilder!* — but as it resonated in her head, another, sharper realization struck her.

If they recognize Liam...

The driver had tied the boat and was already helping Regan and her friend ashore. Liam and Azure were behind them, Liam reaching back to hold Azure's hand as he climbed. Ignoring the rolling of the waves, Tara crossed the boat in three strides and stepped onto the platform behind them.

Voices above, louder. Movement.

Tara climbed, wanting her feet on solid ground. Azure and Liam had reached the top. Two more steps, one more.

Liam's voice, low and tight.

"Oh, shit."

And Tara's vision was engulfed in a flash of white light.

Chapter Six

For a moment there was nothing but voices and light.

"Mr Wilder! Can we get a comment on...?"

A microphone thrust into her face like a club.

"Mrs Wilder! Azure! How long will you be in Spain?"

Her skin prickled—sweat tickled her face. Azure took a deep breath and reached for Liam's arm.

It was all so fast, so loud. Voices on top of voices, overlapping and building into an unbreachable wall of sound, and closer, always coming closer.

Look left, the rock wall. Look right, the railing and a steep drop to the sea. Nowhere to go.

The heat was overwhelming. Liam's shoulder appeared in her line of sight—he had stepped in front of her, a partial barrier, but not enough, oh God, not enough, and the noise was closing in, her breath roaring in her ears—

Her chest was constricting. Damn it, she couldn't *breathe*.

It was worse than Tara had imagined.

The entire walkway seemed to be full of jostling reporters. Colored shirts, faces, hair in a seething mass, flecked with the black of cameras or microphones, all surged and fell around *him* and her sister.

Liam had moved forward, wearing the straight-backed square-shouldered stance of the professional. His presence was pushing back the first wave — of course it was. He was their main interest — he would hold their attention.

And they were holding his.

Azure was directly ahead of Tara. Her shoulders were heaving, fingers clenching at her sides. Azure's head turned to the side, sharply, as though she were scanning for an escape route, and Tara moved forward, one arm outstretched, ready to catch her shoulder and pull her aside.

Then she saw two rogue journalists flanking, breaking formation to dart forward.

The first one Liam grabbed, forcing him back — the second took advantage and pushed past, microphone in his leading hand. Before Tara could move, Azure stepped backwards onto her foot and, caught off balance, stumbled toward the rock wall. The movement exposed her to the sight of the horde, and Tara could see a third, and fourth, preparing to follow their fellow member. Their rush forward took Liam by surprise and, with a swift glance, Tara realized that he was cut off.

It was down to her.

More movement, more pushing, and Azure was jostled against the wall, her eyes flaring wide like a cornered fox. Darting forward, Tara blocked one reporter with an outstretched palm to the chest and caught her sister's arm, but Azure's face had taken on that vacant look Tara remembered from years ago.

When she first came home from her deployment, lying on the sofa all day and never moving, never talking.

Suddenly Azure had jerked free of Tara's grip and surged forward, striking out desperately. One man fell back, but his photographer still loomed, and before Tara could stop her Azure had collided forcefully with his camera.

A gasp of pain, a sudden flash of blood.

Tara pulled Azure against her, tucking her sister's face into the crook of her neck. Warm wetness began to creep down her shoulder, and she clenched her teeth.

I have to get her out of here.

She caught Liam's panicked eyes and revised her thought.

We have *to get her out of here.*

A hand landed on her arm from behind and Ryan's voice was close to her ear. "Get behind me."

Without waiting for an answer, he was suddenly in front of her, forcing his way through the crowd. Tara followed in his wake as Ryan strode forward, the crowd parting around him. She tightened her grip on Azure, who was stumbling, and forced herself to look straight ahead, ignoring the flashes that were still going off around her.

Liam appeared on Azure's other side and Tara suppressed a jolt as his hand landed on the small of her back, his other hand resting on Azure's shoulder. Together, lurching, they reached the edge of the crowd where path met sand and continued toward the main road.

Her neck sticky with blood and her back tingling at *his* contact, Tara wondered again what the hell she was doing here.

Then Ryan was waving, a taxi waiting alongside him, and relief flooded through Tara's every nerve.

* * * *

The hospital waiting room was clean, green and smelled of liniment and bleach.

Nobody was speaking, the air oppressive. Tara held a Catalan newspaper in front of her like a shield, feigning interest in the copy. The building was air conditioned, and goose bumps were forming on the bare skin of her arms and legs.

She cast a glance at *him*.

Liam was staring vacantly at the wall across from him, his brow creased, mouth half open as though about to speak. He was sitting almost bolt upright, very still, very straight, hands resting on his knees. He had been in that pose for the best part of an hour, unmoving, except for occasional glances toward the door.

Azure had vanished through that door in the presence of a brisk, suntanned nurse, who had spoken quietly in Spanish with Liam before leaving. Tara had caught the word 'sutura' and had inwardly winced. She knew enough Spanish to guess what that meant.

It could have been so much worse.

Her neck, now freshly washed, prickled at the touch of her damp hair and an image, a memory, came into her head — Azure with that hideous gash over her eye, her olive cheek mottled with glistening blood.

Azure lying bloodied and broken on the sun-bleached ground, uniform torn, a dust-cloud engulfing her.

Damn it. How does she make me feel sorry for her?

The air grew heavier.

Tara wrenched her eyes from Liam and looked across to the window, where Ryan was casually reclining, gazing into the gardens. As if sensing her scrutiny, he caught Tara's eye and winked.

Tara bit her lip hard. *I am not going to laugh. I am not.*

But she could feel her mouth twitching, and it was ridiculous, because it wasn't even *funny* — and a muscle jerked in her calf, another in her wrist, and the wave of hysteria was becoming overwhelming.

Get up. Go outside. Move.

Tara got up and left.

The corridor outside was spacious, empty. She leaned her head against the cool expanse of wall and wrestled with her composure.

Damn it, I haven't come that close to losing it since —

Azure wild-eyed and frantic, tearing at the air. Azure's lean, stiffened body lying uncomfortably on the sofa. Azure radiant in white, smiling from the front page of a tabloid newspaper, under a blaring headline.

Tara locked her fingers together and fought to breathe.

"Tara." Ryan's voice, somewhere behind her shoulder. When had he followed her out? Tara stiffened, tried to straighten, but a hand fell lightly on the back of her neck, sending a disconcerting thrill along the ridge of her spine.

"It's all right." The voice was low, steady. "She's going to be fine."

"I'm okay," Tara mumbled, cursing herself for sounding quavery.

Fingers began massaging her neck. "Relax."

"I am relaxed."

"It's okay to be worried, you know."

You don't know anything, Tara thought, her body unwillingly growing limp under the rhythmic motions. *You don't know why I didn't speak to her in two years. You don't know how she looked when she came home that last time. I have no right to be worried about her.*

And I can't let myself lose it like this.

Straightening her spine, she let her head fall back, unwittingly releasing a soft sigh of pleasure. The hand on her neck stilled momentarily then continued its movements.

Interesting.

"Is that better?"

Ryan's voice had taken on a deeper tone, and something comfortably familiar snapped into place. This she could do. This game she could play.

An image of Liam drifted into her head, holding her in his arms and whispering words of comfort.

Is that better?

Rolling her shoulders, Tara allowed a smile to cross her face, holding the vision in her head.

"Much better."

"Good."

Ryan kept working his fingers, and Tara arched her back like a cat, closing her eyes.

"I knew I could make you relax."

The smug note in his voice made Tara frown briefly before censoring her expression.

"I'm quite flattered really."

Grr. The vision of Liam was starting to dissipate, and Tara ground her teeth. This idiot was doing his best to destroy her fantasy.

"You took charge today to protect your sister. I like that." A low chuckle. "I like to take charge too."

The words *'Get behind me'* echoed in Tara's head. With a swift, steadying breath, she snapped round and faced Ryan squarely.

"I'm sure you do. But not of me."

She turned away and strode back down the corridor toward the waiting room, forcing the blank mask back onto her face.

It took the sight of the immobile, immoveable Liam to erase the memory of Ryan's closing smirk from her head.

* * * *

The coastline of Tossa de Mar vanished behind the headland with the finality of a sigh of relief.

Azure leaned on Liam's shoulder, her dark hair pushed back to reveal an ugly row of sutures from eyebrow to temple. Liam was talking to her in a low voice that carried across the space between them and Tara. Watching the waves, Tara kept her face turned away but her ear turned toward them.

"Let's go get some lunch when we get back on. Maybe they'll have those sausages with oregano again." A pause. "I hope so."

A soft giggle from Azure. "You know they will. They'd do sausages with caviar if you asked them."

"Hmm, I might ask."

There was a light thud, which Tara interpreted as a friendly slap from Azure.

"As long as it's not that *awful* lumpfish."

"Hmm." Azure's voice took on a wry note. "For you? Tracey would ship in the best. Red *and* black."

"I'm honored."

Despite the persistent ache in her neck, Tara kept her face turned resolutely away, shielding her expression behind her hair. It just didn't sound *right* to hear Liam Wilder's soft, slightly fey voice discussing his favorite sausages.

Let alone being fussy about his caviar.

The slap of the waves grew louder as the vast wall of the yacht loomed. Looking up, Tara could see a row of unclear faces populating the heights of the railing. Even here Azure was the center of attention, and Tara's mask slipped back into place as they drew closer to the boat.

She wondered if the others had continued their shore leave or had been taken straight back to the yacht. Had the press dispersed after the taxi had left, or pushed for interviews with the other passengers? And how would this affect their itinerary? Would they stay on the Spanish coast?

Tracey might know. Tara resolved to ask.

Regan's wide, eager eyes were visible over the rail as the tender was tied and the four disembarked. Tara steeled herself as she reached the top of the steps, expecting any moment either to be bombarded with questions or thrust aside so that Azure could be interrogated.

A hand landed on her shoulder from behind.

"Tara."

Turning, she came face to face with Azure. At the same time a prickle in her back told her that someone — probably Regan or Kiki — had come up behind her.

"Azure."

It was a stiff response, but *fuck*. Nothing had prepared her for this situation. The coldness of estrangement mingled with the reawakened role of sister and rescuer, and damn it, she had no idea what to say.

From the look of uncertain determination on her face, neither did Azure, but she pressed on.

"I want to talk to you." She glanced over Tara's shoulder. "Not here."

Wordless, Tara gave a brief nod.

"After lunch. Say about two on the upper deck, where the tables are."

For a moment Tara paused, but she knew it was mostly a front. If they were to be on the yacht for two months, they couldn't spend that time avoiding each other. They needed to talk.

"Okay."

Azure held her gaze for a long moment, then nodded coolly and abruptly left her. Tara turned her head automatically to follow her as she moved to join Liam, who was leaning on one of the lifebelts watching her.

Not Azure. Watching *her*.

And with a strange look in his eyes and an inscrutable smile that grew slightly as she stared, an unfamiliar glittery feeling forming in the pit of her stomach.

Why was he watching her? Did he remember her now? Did he—

Oh God, Liam...

Azure reached his side. Liam turned to face her, and they were gone.

The tension in the air was immediately broken by Regan, who appeared from behind, wanting to know all the details of the hospital visit. "Was Azure badly hurt? Was she concussed? Are they going to sue?"

Kiki hovered behind, her sardonic smile suggesting that her previous lethargy had fled, and Tara allowed herself to be led away to the dining room, answering questions and privately thankful that Regan's babble and Kiki's occasional comments left her no time for dwelling on circumstances.

Ryan's lascivious smile, as she passed him, told her exactly what he was thinking.

What Liam had been thinking remained to be seen.

Chapter Seven

"So what did she say?"

"She said yes." Azure threw her bag down on the bed and turned to face Liam, who was locking the cabin door. "So we'll see what happens."

"She looked really worried about you earlier." Liam sat down on the bed and kicked his shoes off.

Azure shrugged uncomfortably. Maybe Tara had been concerned and maybe she hadn't, but either way this wasn't a conversation she was looking forward to. Her sister wasn't known for making these things easy.

"I'm going to take a shower. My hair is full of crap."

"Hold on. I'll help you. You can't see your sutures."

Azure nodded. It was true enough. The last thing she wanted was to break her stitches and end up back in hospital. Or get soap in them and have them stinging for ages. Bloodied hair was hanging in her eyes, stiff and unpleasant, a reminder of what had happened today. She just wanted it over.

And the prospect of a shower with Liam was always welcome.

When they returned from the en suite twenty minutes later, Azure wrapped in a towel, the room had cooled slightly. As Azure reached for the hairdryer she noticed goose bumps rising on her arms, the tiny hairs standing on end.

"Jesus. How can it be roasting out there and cold in here? Their air con is amazing."

"I hadn't noticed." Liam threw his towel onto a chair. "Move around a bit. That'll warm you up."

Azure heard a thud behind her and turned to see Liam dancing elegantly around the room, stark naked. She folded her arms and bit her lip to stifle her laughter.

"And is it working?"

"I don't know, I wasn't cold. Join me and find out."

Azure shook her head indulgently. *What the hell?* She untucked her towel and let it fall, leaving her as naked as him. Liam held out his hand and she took it, moving into his arms as he led her into a tango.

"You're nuts. You do realize that, don't you?"

"Of course. Everyone should go nuts once in a while. Makes life more interesting." Liam spun her, sending her wet hair in a sparkling circle, droplets falling all over the floor.

Azure collapsed into giggles, letting Liam take the lead as they danced around the room. As they passed the floor-length mirror she caught a glimpse of herself and bit back a gasp, catching a brief impression of her flushed bare arse, rose-pink nipples and a dusting of dark hair.

"See," Liam said, sweeping her into his arms and dipping her. "I told you it would warm you up." He leaned down and pressed a kiss between her breasts.

Oh.

As she straightened up, Azure slid closer to him, pressing her body against his. Liam dropped his hand from her back to her bottom and cupped one cheek, letting one finger drift inwards to graze against the hidden pucker.

Azure's eyes widened. *Oh, really? Two can play that game.* She brushed a hip against Liam's crotch, at the same time reaching down to caress his cock.

As Liam kept them moving, it became a battle of wills. Their bodies brushed together teasingly, hands slipping into intimate places, touching each other until they were breathless. Azure glided behind him and wrapped her arms around his chest, caressing his nipples with her fingertips. Turning on the spot, Liam pulled Azure against him and pressed a hand to her pussy, sliding a finger inside as his thumb caressed her clit.

Azure tipped her head back and kissed him, letting her tongue slide into his mouth as she laced her fingers behind his neck.

Their lips parted, and Liam said two words.

"Hold still."

And he slid his hands under her bottom and lifted her up before placing her on top of the desk.

Azure squealed at the coldness of the varnished wood against her skin. She hooked her ankles together behind Liam's back, gripping his shoulders. She dropped her head back as his cock entered her, before she let out a moan as he slid inside her to the hilt.

Liam set a rapid pace, lowering his head to whisper in her ear as their bodies rocked together.

"We're going to do this again after you've spoken to Tara."

"Yes." Azure clung to him as her jewelry box fell over, spilling necklaces and rings across the desk.

"Slowly."

"Yes."

"I'm going to lay you out on the bed and suck your toes, one by one, licking them until you can't stand it anymore."

"Yes." Azure stifled a moan in his shoulder. Beside her, the carriage clock toppled and rolled onto the floor with a thud.

"I'm going to take the lube and prepare you with it in that way you like—remember?"

Azure nodded, biting down on her lip. She remembered. That time Liam had flipped her onto her stomach, slid three fingers into her narrowest channel and teased her for long minutes as she lay there, aching with need, before—

"And then I'll stroke you *here*"—he moved his hand from her leg to her pussy, two fingers caressing her clit—"as I take you."

As he had taken her before—entering her arse with one slow thrust, first moving gently, not wanting to hurt, then faster and faster as his fingers had worked her clit, until she had screamed his name.

"Liam!"

As she cried out and shuddered, Liam crushed her against him and thrust hard, once, twice, three times before groaning deeply with his climax.

For a long time they stayed in place, silently supporting each other as their breathing slowed and their bodies cooled. Azure rested her head on Liam's shoulder, her legs hanging limply off the desk as Liam stroked her hair.

"I think I need another shower," she said finally.

Liam laughed, lifting her chin to look her in the eye. "No you don't. You're fine."

Azure twisted her mouth wryly. "I'm not sure I want to meet Tara looking freshly fucked."

"From what you said, she's seen it often enough in the mirror, so it shouldn't shock her."

Azure nodded, acknowledging the truth of this. Of course, Liam didn't know the whole story. He had no idea of Tara's obsession, or how she might react to the evidence of their sex life.

In fact, Azure wasn't sure herself how Tara would react. It wasn't likely to be good. If Tara had ignored her for two years for daring to get married, the crime of having sex would probably give her a conniption.

Still, she had come on the trip. She had agreed to talk with her. And she had helped to rescue her from those fucking paparazzi.

God, if Tara hadn't been there, if Tara hadn't dragged her away...

At the memory, she shivered. Liam noticed.

"Are you cold? You'd better get dressed."

"No, no, I'm fine—although you're right, I should." Azure eased herself off the desk, which had stuck to her skin and peeled off unpleasantly. "I was thinking of the paps today."

Liam's eyes darkened. "Don't remind me."

"How did they find us? I thought we were on full security?"

"We are. I'm just going to have to increase it even further. There has to be a leak somewhere." Liam stared off into the distance for a moment, thinking. "I'll speak to Nik. He understands how important this is."

Azure nodded.

"I'll get ready and we can go get some lunch."

"Sure." Liam pressed a kiss to her forehead before turning toward the wardrobe. "Don't forget the sunscreen."

"I won't."

Although, Azure thought as she retrieved the hairdryer, if the worst thing that happened today was sunburn, she would go to bed a happy girl.

Chapter Eight

The upper deck was a suntrap, the hot metal of the seats uncomfortable in the blaze of warm light. Tara sat at a table near the bar, back stiff, her hands clasped around a Tequila Sunrise topped with a pink umbrella.

"You're early," said a voice behind her. A leafy mojito slid into view, closely followed by Azure, who dropped into the opposite seat with exaggerated lassitude. Her makeup had been freshly reapplied and her hair was pulled back, almost flaunting the row of stitches over her eye.

"I'm always early."

Something flickered in Azure's eyes, to be immediately stifled. She leaned in to sip from her straw before turning back to Tara with an air of purpose.

"Look, I just wanted to thank you for what you did."

Tara nodded stiffly. "How long has that been going on?"

"Oh, since the start. We can't go anywhere without shit like that. We thought we'd kept it secret this time, but..." Azure bit her lip and shrugged awkwardly. "Well you know how it is. They get hold of everything. Like when they got hold of —"

Her voice broke off. Tara had heard it as clear as day — *Like when they got hold of the engagement.* The bold headline, the hyperbolic text, the blurry, stolen photograph.

The first nail in the coffin.

Tara took a gulp from her cocktail as the band round her stomach tightened.

"So," Azure said after a moment, "when did you get back to England?"

"Last week."

"Long tour?"

"Six months."

The same ripple of distaste crossed Azure's face, and Tara's temper flared.

"Don't act like it's such a bad thing. You were in the Army too. *Once.*"

"Oh, like I even had any choice." Azure turned away, her eyes shuttering, and Tara recognized the signs of withdrawal, but the bait was too hard to ignore.

"Of course you had a choice. You could have —"

Eyes like lasers spun back to face her, boring into her own.

"I could have what, exactly? I suggested joining the RAF once and Dad nearly skinned me alive. He didn't even like me being in the Air Corps —" Azure gripped the edge of the table, the effort of stopping herself clear. "Being discharged was the best damn thing that ever happened to me."

Tara opened her mouth to defend her father — *He didn't force us, he didn't force me, I could have done anything I wanted* — but then her thoughts whirled as Azure's last words hit home.

'Being discharged was the best thing that ever happened to me.'

And then she married him.

And it hurt, the reminder hurt so *much*, and the image of herself as a family-whipped military drone compared to rebellious, happily married Azure was too much to bear, grating at her control like sandpaper.

"Oh, was it? I happen to like the Army, thank you." She heard her voice come out raw, bitter. "But then you wouldn't care about that, would you? Heaven forbid you give a shit how anyone else feels."

The barb was thrown, and she saw with satisfaction Azure's eyes narrow as it struck.

So we've finally got to this, have we?

Azure had known that Tara would make this difficult. From the moment she had seen her at the table, early as usual, her sister had radiated discomfort, rejection. *Get back. Keep away.* Every inch of her was stiff, poised, fiercely controlled.

And now the veneer was cracking.

"I didn't know the press had got it. I tried to call…"

Tara let out an irritated huff of breath.

"You wouldn't talk to me!" Azure exclaimed. "I didn't mean for you to find out like that—"

"You wouldn't understand," Tara spat, then abruptly looked away, skin flushing.

Azure wondered if Tara realized how innately childish those last words had sounded.

And surely that was the point. Because this was all down to that *fucking* crush Tara had nursed, wasn't it?

Even though it had been years ago.

Even though it had all been over and done with until Azure had dared to—

"You're damn right," Azure snapped back, feeling her face contort even as she fought down her anger. "I *don't* understand."

Tara still avoided her eyes.

"You were a kid. It was a crush. You don't even have it anymore. What's the…"

"That is not the damn point."

Tara's blush had increased inexplicably, and Azure found herself staring, even though Tara's face had twisted into a mask of—fury?

Hate?

"What is the point then?"

"You knew…" Tara began, then broke off, biting her lip.

'You knew how I'd feel?' 'You knew it would hurt me?' Azure waited for a moment, watching the emotions warring for control over Tara's face, hoping for some kind of insight. Something. Anything.

I can't fix this if you won't talk to me.

But the battle ceased, and the mask fell, and Tara's eyes returned to hers, anger glazed with ice.

Azure could have screamed with frustration.

"This is fucking ridiculous. I'm not going to make a decision like that based on some total fantasy you…"

"It wasn't even based on a *total* week." Tara's emphasis on the *total* was accompanied by a jeering false accent. *Toadal.* "Don't tell me you sat down and made a decision."

Of course. Tara who didn't do relationships, Tara who never rushed into anything without hours of planning. The concept of falling in love, of a whirlwind romance, had to be beyond her.

Sat down and made a decision? There had been no decision to make. Liam had asked, and she had known.

It had been on the Friday morning. Sitting at the little marble table on the patio, eating breakfast. Her food had been untouched in front of her, her fingers beating a staccato tattoo on the table, stomach bound so tightly it had displaced her heart.

Liam had barely begun his own meal, had taken only a few unnaturally relaxed bites before laying down his fork.

"It's Friday," he had said casually, his voice so soft she had wanted to weep. "Is it time for you to go?"

Azure's inner voice had screamed *no* even as her throat had clenched. She had stilled her fingers, taken a deep breath and forced herself to speak.

"*Is* it time for me to go?"

"No." The word had been bitten off.

Her heart had jolted.

Liam had reached across the table, took her hands in his.

"Don't go." A breathless pause. "I love you."

For a moment Azure had thought that she would never breathe again. Her words had come out almost as a convulsion.

"Then I won't."

And she never had, and when he had followed his pronouncement with "Will you marry me?" her answer had needed no thought. She was staying with Liam—all else had gone without saying, and nothing else was of any importance—not the wedding planning, not the logistics of moving to the US, nothing.

She had thrown everything away for love, and hadn't regretted it once.

But explaining that to Tara would be impossible.

"You don't plan these things," she said finally. "They just happen."

Tara shook her head, dismissal in the motion, and Azure's anger flared sharply.

"Why can't you just be glad I'm happy?"

"Oh, please." An ugly sneer twisted Tara's face. "I didn't even know you were unhappy, except for when you came home all PTSD'd."

It was out of her mouth before she'd been able to stop it.

Azure stared at her, dazed, her mouth hanging open, and Tara caught her breath, her mind frantically searching for a way to take the words back.

There was none.

"I—"

I saw what was wrong and I ignored it.

I had to hit you where it hurt the most.

"You f—" Azure began, before stopping herself with visible effort. Biting her lip, she stood to leave, shaking her head as if to say that Tara was beyond all hope.

"Wait." *Maybe I can —*

"No." Azure held up a hand, and Tara fell silent. "*No.* Now you listen."

Tara held her body still, steadying herself for the onslaught, before jerking backwards in shock as Azure slammed both hands down on the table and leaned in to face her.

"You know *nothing* about what happened to me out there," Azure spat, her eyes boring like gimlets into Tara's. "You know *nothing* about me and Liam, or why I married him. And you never will, because you won't ever understand."

Her breath hit Tara's face like a slap.

"You won't understand because you can't. You can't understand anything that didn't happen to you. And it will never happen to you, what happened to me with Liam, because you're such a cold-hearted fucking bitch that no one would ever fall for you."

Azure straightened, casting Tara a look of pure ice.

"I don't even know why I bothered."

And, pausing only to catch up the mojito that still stood on the table, she turned her back on Tara and stalked away. Her last words floated back to Tara over her shoulder.

"You're so not worth it."

* * * *

"Pull."

Swish.

Crack.

The clay exploded in mid-air, showering the ocean with broken pieces. Without shifting her stance, Tara cocked the shotgun again.

"Pull."

Swish. Another clay pigeon soared into view.

Crack. It disintegrated. Tara lowered the gun and began to reload it with swift, jerky movements.

Cold-hearted fucking bitch.

Two months of this. Two fucking months.

She snapped the gun closed and raised it to take aim.

"P—"

"Who're you trying to kill?" said someone behind her.

Tara jumped, firing a shot into the air.

"Fuck!"

"Sorry." The owner of the voice had moved to her side, and, letting the gun hang down, Tara turned to see that it was Kiki.

"Don't *do* that! I could have…"

Kiki held up both hands. "Relax. You didn't."

Tara bit back an angry response and took a deep breath, forcing herself to calm down. "Sorry. It's been a long day."

"It has," Kiki agreed. "How's Azure doing?"

"As you'd expect."

"Hmm." Kiki paused. "Pity we didn't get to see Tossa de Mar. I had to spend the afternoon in the bar with Regan. I love her, but God, she never shuts up."

Tara made a noncommittal noise. She had gathered from Regan that the others had returned immediately to the boat to avoid the press. It was just as well, really. The thought of Regan in front of a microphone was enough to turn her stomach.

"It probably shook her up."

"Yeah, but then she got a call from one of her friends who's dating a married man, and I got a monologue on the evils of adultery. I nearly had to choke her with a straw."

Laughing, Tara lifted the gun to her eye again. Kiki stepped back and waited in silence as the pigeon soared before being scattered to the wind.

"Good shot."

"Thanks." Tara laid down the gun. "So where's Regan now?"

"Went to her room to call her friend back." Kiki rolled her expressive eyes. "Fuss about nothing in my view. If a married man wanted to date me, I wouldn't say no."

Tara raised her eyebrows. "Oh? Why not?"

Kiki cast her a slit-eyed look. "I'm sure you'd see that as home-wrecking, right?"

Cocking her head, Tara coolly held her gaze.

"Well, I don't. He's the one breaking his vows, not me. If he loved his wife he wouldn't do it, and if he doesn't, she should find someone who does." Kiki gave a casual shrug. "The mistress is the catalyst, that's all."

"You've really given this some thought, haven't you?"

Seeing that Kiki was ready to go, Tara decided to follow. It was only a few hours before dinner and her clothes were heavy with sweat, clinging to her uncomfortably. Kiki gave a short laugh as they turned to leave.

"You try listening to Regan ravin' and see how far you get. In fact, you can do that at dinner tonight."

"Oh, go on. She's not that bad."

"I'm glad you think so," was Kiki's airy response. "Because I won't be there. I've got other plans tonight."

"*What?*"

* * * *

Sitting alone at the table, a menu pinched tightly between thumb and forefinger, Tara thought of Kiki again and ground her teeth.

'Other plans' indeed.

"I'm spending the evening in the spa," Kiki had casually replied when Tara had asked. "They do a detox program. I get a full body massage and then they bring me a salad."

Bypassing the description of the salon as a 'spa', Tara had been unconvinced, but had stayed silent.

Whatever Kiki was doing, she clearly didn't want anyone to know.

Which left her spending dinner staring at an empty chair.

Damn.

Turning her attention back to the menu, she ran an eye down the list of dishes, raising an eyebrow as she reached the desserts. A surprising number of items were familiar to her.

Bolognese stuffed pasta shells
Tom yam goong
Oeuf en meurette
~
Rainbow trout
Double-baked cheese soufflé
Kobe steak with caprese salad
~
Lime cheesecake
Peach cobbler
Lemon meringue pie

Almost every dish on the menu was either a favorite of hers or Azure's.

Carefully keeping her face straight, Tara slid her eyes sideways toward the Sugiyamas' table. Tracey was already resident and also facing an empty chair, a look of discontent on her face that boded ill for her tardy husband.

She could understand why Azure's favorites were on the menu. Quite so many was unusual, but still… She found herself wondering again why so many of *hers* would be there.

How would they even know? Had Azure…

Her back prickled uncomfortably, and Tara automatically twisted round in her seat, but no one was there. The movement brought another table into view, this one empty, and an image of Azure and Liam flitted into her head. Azure and Liam, dressing for dinner, husband and wife, talking about their day.

Azure telling him about their argument—Liam's face darkening in anger, disappointment.

No. Tara inwardly winced. *I have to make this right.*

That prickling again, and this time as Tara turned, she felt a pointed tap on her opposite shoulder. Snapping back around, she immediately met a flat stomach in lime green silk, framed in tailored black and accentuated with a hunter green tie. Even as she followed its line upwards, she knew whose face she would find at the top.

Well, at least it wasn't Reese. She had managed to avoid him so far.

"Surprise, Golden Girl."

Tara allowed herself to smile, forcing down the roiling in her stomach. "Hi, Ryan. Are you on your own too?"

Ryan rested his hand on the back of her chair as he returned her smile, leaning down to face her.

"Not anymore." A slight arch of the eyebrow. "Kiki happened to mention you'd be dining alone tonight and…" He tilted his blond head toward the empty chair. "Asked me to join you."

Before Tara could respond, Ryan had moved from behind her and seated himself opposite her, reclining and stretching with supreme confidence in his position. She could already see the waiter approaching as though he had been waiting for her date to arrive.

"Oh, you've got to be fucking *kidding* me!"

Chapter Nine

"Here. Have a drink." Ryan filled Tara's glass with red wine and pushed it across the table. "You look like you need it."

Oh boy, do I need it. Tara drained the glass in one gulp then handed it back to him. If she was going to have to spend the evening in Ryan's company, she had no intention of doing so sober.

I will murder Kiki, she promised herself.

Ryan seemed entirely oblivious to her mood. Either that or he was choosing to ignore it. In the amount of time—mercifully brief—it had taken between the placing of orders and the arrival of the merlot, he had managed to keep the conversation to casual small talk. Did she know where Kiki was? *'No.'* Had she tried the clay pigeon shooting yet? *'Yes, earlier.'* Was she a good shot? *'I never miss.'*

The potential threat in that last statement had led to a raised eyebrow and a smile that Tara found herself unable to resist returning. Well, it was a smile. She could let him have a smile.

But God, she was in no mood for games tonight.

"Oh, *great,*" Ryan said with feeling, glancing over Tara's shoulder. "The appetisers are here. I'm starved."

"Me too."

The waiter's hand appeared in front of her with a plate of stuffed pasta shells, and Tara found it impossible to suppress a soft sigh of approval. The warm aroma of bolognese sauce almost made her shiver with anticipation.

"I see you like your food," Ryan commented, his face partially behind a veil of rising steam from his soup. "I can't stand women who think starvation is healthy."

"Oh really?"

"Yeah, really." Ryan's tone was lightly mocking, as if daring her to find offense. "Far smarter to eat like a regular person and keep fit in the gym. It works for us, right?"

Tara eyed him for a moment, considering. "Right."

Without further comment, Ryan turned his attention to his food, leaving Tara to muse on her situation as she cut into the first shell. Maybe this would be easier than she'd thought.

Maybe he would even serve as a distraction.

A third glass and a fourth followed. As the main courses arrived, along with a second bottle of merlot, a permanent smile had glued itself to Tara's face, the warmth of the wine flowing through her body and heating her skin.

Having dinner with Ryan was surprisingly pleasant. He was easy on the eye and didn't interrupt her while she was eating, even if he did have that slight smirk of a smile that suggested he could read her mind.

And even that was somehow less irritating now.

"So tell me," Ryan said, looking up from his meal, "how come you haven't been to see Azure in the last two years?"

And with those words, the pleasant haze vanished.

"How do you know I haven't?"

"She introduced you to Liam right in front of me."

Bugger. A faint memory of that first evening flashed through Tara's mind.

"I've been deployed."

"The whole time?"

Tara considered lying for a moment before deciding against it. "No. But I was only home for a month or so at a time, and I didn't want to spend that time traveling."

There. That should shut him up.

Ryan, apparently satisfied, turned back to his food, and Tara relaxed. Hopefully that would be the only awkward moment of the evening.

"How did she meet Liam, anyway?"

Ugh.

There was no point in pleading ignorance. Anyone who knew the story — Kiki, for instance, or Azure and Liam themselves — could contradict her, and any attempt at obfuscation would only look suspicious. The thought of Ryan — of *anyone* — guessing the truth made her inwardly cringe.

"She entered a competition."

Ryan looked up, interest lighting his eyes. "To meet Liam? Really?"

"Yeah." Tara ignored the familiar pain in her stomach. "Really."

* * * *

Two years earlier

It was shortly after Tara's arrival home, during Azure's recuperation.

Azure was going through a 'competition' phase. Every magazine, every newspaper, every prize-winning crossword or silly piece of advertising had to be filled in, even if the prize was nothing anyone would want. Tara ignored it—her parents indulged it.

Then it had been on the radio.

"Have you heard this one, Tara?"

Azure looked up at her as Tara walked into the living room. She was curled up on the sofa in her usual position, notepad in hand and looking brighter than Tara had seen her in days.

"Are you still doing those bloody things? You're never actually going to win anything."

Azure waved her dismissal away. "Miserable bitch. Listen to this. Complete the following sentence to win an all expenses paid weekend at the Land of Light, California, staying in the east wing of Liam Wilder's personal mansion. 'I want to visit the Land of Light because...'"

"'I need my head examined'," Tara finished dryly, ignoring the sudden leap her heart had made at the mention of Liam Wilder.

It was ridiculous. The chances of winning were astronomical.

And yet a tiny part of her was screaming, *Do it! Do it! You might win!*

"You should enter it, Tara." Azure looked at her knowingly. Of course, she had no idea that Tara had met him already. "It'd be cool."

"It'd be pointless," Tara insisted. "All the way to California for one weekend? Do you have any idea how long that flight is? And anyway, what kind of stupid sentence is that? How is anyone supposed to answer that and be original?"

It was a question that Tara had pondered for a long time afterwards. She had never bothered to ask Azure what she had written as her answer.

In fact, she didn't even know that Azure had entered it until the phone call.

Coming back into the house from the base grocery store, she found Azure in the kitchen with their mother, midway through an excited monologue, the cordless phone still clutched in her hand.

"...can't *believe* it!"

"What can't you believe?" Tara asked.

Azure spun round to face her, wide-eyed and glowing. "That competition to win a trip to the Land of Light? I won!"

The room swayed under Tara's feet.

"*What?*"

"I know, I can't believe it either." Azure shook her head, hair in a black flurry, as Tara struggled to regain her scattered wits. "It's been ages since I went to a theme park, too. And California…"

Fuck the theme park! Fuck California! You're going to see Liam Wilder instead of me!

But Tara bit her tongue and forced a smile onto her face as Azure's dizzying babble continued.

Why hadn't she entered?

Why?

There were a million reasons. Because she never entered competitions. Because she wouldn't have won anyway. Because she was twenty-four and a lieutenant in the Army, not some screaming freak.

But somehow, now, they all sounded like excuses.

Arrangements were made, and Tara bit her tongue as Azure prepared to fly out, forcing her feelings down. It would all be over soon.

Then the day came.

Bags packed, Azure popped her head round Tara's bedroom door on her way down the stairs.

"Not going to say goodbye?"

"You're going away for the weekend," Tara responded coolly. "You're not being posted abroad."

Azure's face crumpled briefly, and Tara bit back an apology, instead moving forward to take Azure's outstretched hand. "I—"

"No, you're right." Azure lowered her eyes for a moment before raising them again, looking Tara full in the face. "Never again."

Of course.

"Why *were* you discharged, anyway?"

"Injuries. Trauma. You know." Azure rolled her eyes expressively.

"But what hap—"

Before Tara could finish, Azure lifted one hand and cut her off abruptly. "Enough. I'm out of here."

Tara nodded, giving Azure's hand one last squeeze. Azure turned to leave, but then paused and looked back, scanning Tara's face with a scrutiny that made her inwardly squirm.

"You're nuts," Azure said finally. "You know nothing's going to happen."

Tara stiffened. For a moment they studied each other, the unmentionable truth hovering between them.

All she could do was acknowledge it.

"I know."

Azure flashed her a quick smile, then ducked her head and left, leaving the door half open. Moments later Tara heard Azure's case bumping down the stairs, across the hall floor and out, the front door closing behind her with a slam.

Nothing's going to happen. Don't be silly.

The first newspaper article was minor, an interior half-column casually noting that Azure Thornton, twenty-four, had arrived at the Land of Light, under a poor photograph of her shaking hands with Liam Wilder. Tara had feigned interest for her parents, ignoring the faintly heavy sensation in her stomach.

She's there to go to the theme park. She probably won't even see him after the handshake.

That was the Saturday morning.

Monday, and a further article had appeared, this time a quarter of a page, stating that Liam Wilder had chosen to extend the prize a further day as he felt a weekend was too little time between such long flights.

The heaviness in Tara's gut grew stronger.

Tuesday, and a half-page, now claiming that the prize had been extended to a week after problems with the flight bookings.

It was ridiculous. Of course it was.

And yet the lethargy that settled over Tara's body as the days passed, the gradual lack of interest in food, the constant tension that made her nights disturbed, told her otherwise.

When Friday's paper hit the mat, the front page headline seemed to have been burnt into her mind for days beforehand.

WILDER TO WED WINNER

In the flurry of activity that followed, Tara retreated to Azure's couch and lay in Azure's languid position, fighting to control the instinct that was pushing her to howl and cry and scream.

I can't. She hasn't. She couldn't. I can't.

"Tara?" Her mother was holding the phone. "Azure wants to talk to you."

The inner animal surfaced just for a moment.

"I'm *not here*."

Tara stood, stalked out of the room, and for the rest of her time at home, her answer never changed.

* * * *

"And I guess they fell in love at first sight."

"I guess they did." Ryan looked mildly surprised, then shrugged and dropped his gaze back to his food.

Tara suppressed an eye roll. Okay, so she hadn't told him the backstory. He had no idea of the protective grip her heart had had on Liam, stupid and immature as it had been, but that had created such a sense of betrayal.

But for fuck's sake, they'd fallen in love after a *week*. A fucking *week!* How was this only worth mild surprise?

Well. Apparently it was.

They finished the meal in silence, broken only by occasional musings on the dessert menu or the wine. As the plates were cleared, Tara glanced over her shoulder to see Azure and Liam finishing their drinks and talking quietly. Her skin prickled at the thought of what Azure might be telling him.

"Do you dance?" came Ryan's voice from behind her.

Tara turned back to face him, flicking her hair out of her face in what she hoped was a casual gesture. "Yeah, I dance."

"Want to?"

What the hell. Made reckless with nerves, Tara threw him a coquettish smile. "Sure. Just give me a minute. I need to ask Azure something."

Ryan made a sweeping motion with his arm. "Go right ahead. I'll be here."

Fighting every impulse to run, Tara forced herself to cross the dining room to Azure's table. Azure looked up in time to see her coming, her eyes widening to add a slightly venomous tinge to her social smile.

Maybe that meant that she hadn't told Liam yet. Tara stopped at their table.

"Could I talk to you for a minute, Azure?"

Azure tilted her head to one side in an innocent movement that didn't fool Tara for one minute. "What about?"

Gah. "I want to apologize."

The smile disappeared from Azure's face. She turned to Liam, who had leaned forward, his face concerned. "I'll be back in a minute."

Well, it was something. Tara followed her sister's curved, satin-clad figure between the tables and out into the corridor, where Azure spun round and fixed her with an icy glare.

"What do you want *really?*"

Tara sighed. "To apologize. Really."

Azure folded her arms, not dropping her gaze.

"Look, what I said earlier — it was wrong of me. And you were right. It's been a long time. And I really don't know anything about you now, or about Liam."

Azure still looked angry, but she unbent enough to give Tara a slow nod.

"I'd like to make up for that."

A long pause, during which Azure scrutinised her with her head on one side, apparently deep in thought. Finally she gave another nod.

"All right. I'll talk to Liam. We're docking offshore at Lloret de Mar tomorrow and going swimming. If he's okay with it, we'll pick you and Kiki up after breakfast."

"All right." A wave of relief flooded Tara's stomach.

Without another word, Azure pushed open the door to the dining room and disappeared through it, leaving Tara to follow.

Ryan was standing at the side of the dance floor when Tara joined him.

"Finished talking?"

"Finished talking." Tara lifted her head and cast him a bold look, holding out her hand. "Let's dance."

With a raised eyebrow, Ryan took her hand and together they walked onto the dance floor.

Tara knew she was a good dancer. She'd been to enough military events to know how to move without embarrassing herself — and to enough nightclubs during leave to know how to rock her hips and undulate her body in a way that drew the eye.

Whether that would work with Ryan was another thing entirely, but hell, he was a man. As Tara turned to face him, she caught the look in his eye and felt a smile kink her mouth.

He watched her like a predator would watch its prey.

A heavy rock number was pulsing through the speakers. Tara moved in close to him, noting with grudging admiration that his rhythm was effortlessly matching hers. He knew how to dance.

And she knew how to flirt.

She turned and felt his body meld with hers, his chest to her back, his hand resting on her hip as they swayed together. Tara let her head fall to the side, exposing her neck. She added a kick to her hips so that her arse brushed against his crotch, smiling to herself as he gasped.

His other arm locked over her shoulder, pulling her closer. She gasped as his breath tickled her ear.

"Want to get some air?"

Against her will, Tara shivered.

"Okay."

Music still blasting, they moved through the crowd to the side door that led to the stairway and up to the deck.

The moment the night air hit them, Ryan turned and pulled Tara against him. Tara tipped her chin up to face him, sliding her arms around his neck, and their lips brushed briefly before his hands caught her waist and his mouth was on hers.

Liam.

She laced her fingers into his hair, stroking the back of his neck. Ryan growled, a low rumble that she could feel in his throat, and a gasp escaped her as Ryan's lips left hers for a second before returning with force, his tongue entwining with hers.

Oh God, Liam…

He slid his hands down her back, cupping the cheeks of her bottom. A wave of heat flooded her stomach and she moaned into his mouth, pressing forward against him as her inner muscles clenched with desire.

No. Not yet.

Steeling herself, she pressed her mouth hard against his before pulling back, fighting to catch her breath.

Ryan moved in for another kiss, but Tara placed her hand on his chest.

"Wait."

"Wait for what?" Ryan's voice was ragged.

Let him think he's weakened you. "I don't..." She lowered her head as if concealing a virginal blush. "I don't do this on the first night."

Ryan stilled, breathing heavily, and Tara allowed herself a moment of triumph. Calling it the first night implied that there would be a second night, made men anticipate the pleasures to come.

And they would come. She knew that now.

But not yet.

"In that case..." He cupped her face with his hands, and she opened her eyes to meet his, his pupils wide with intensity as Ryan spoke, "I'd better let you go back to your room, right?"

"Right." Tara laughed softly, partially out of relief. She moved back farther, meaning to leave, but Ryan's arms tightened around her and he pulled her in for another hard, savage kiss, his hands jerking upwards to clench in her hair.

As he released her, she staggered and heard his low chuckle.

"I'll see you tomorrow."

"Yeah." Tara threw her hair back and straightened up to her full height. "Tomorrow."

She could still hear him laughing as she rounded the stern.

The deck on this side was deserted but for one figure, who appeared in front of Tara just as her hand reached the door handle.

It was Kiki, looking as disheveled and kiss-smudged as Tara felt.

Kiki looked Tara up and down, taking in every misplaced hair and smear of makeup, and silently raised an eyebrow. Coolly, Tara regarded Kiki's own condition and raised one back.

"Okay," said Kiki after a moment. "I won't tell if you don't."

"Deal."

Immediately on entering their room, Kiki disappeared into the bathroom, locking the door behind her. Tara swiftly undressed, hung up her dress then put her shoes away in the wardrobe before sitting down on the edge of the bed. For a moment she watched the bathroom door, waiting for Kiki to emerge.

Then she heard the shower running.

She opened the drawer in the bedside cabinet and looked down at the photograph that lay on top of her underwear.

Liam Wilder.

With one ear tuned to the sound of the shower, Tara reached up to switch the light off and slid into bed, already sliding one hand down over her stomach.

That business with Ryan had left her frustrated. Time to relieve the tension.

Oh.

She closed her eyes as she teased her folds with her fingers, softly sliding one inside herself as her breath quickened.

Liam.

Pressing the heel of her hand down hard on her clit, she moved it in circles, stifling a moan as her pleasure began to mount. She slipped a second finger inside and clenched down onto it, picturing Liam thrusting into her, his hands everywhere, cupping her breasts, her arse—

The shower continued to run, and as Tara arched her back on the mattress, as she moved her fingers, tormenting and stroking until finally, finally she bit her lip and gasped in completion, she screamed *Liam* in her head and never let loose a sound.

* * * *

Running, running, always running. Dodging flying wreckage from deafening explosions, the ground rocking beneath her. Barely able to see, Azure was moving only on instinct.

There was no escape. This time it was all over.

Then a crack, a sudden hard blow to the back, and the ground came up to meet her, pain rippling from a spot over her kidney.

Shot.

Looking up through the dust, eyes tearing, sun dazzling, she saw a figure standing before her, face impassive under a mane of blonde hair. Conscious of blood leaking onto the ground, sticky against her skin, she reached up with one hand. Help me.

But the figure simply stood and stared down at her, coolly unaffected, until she woke.

Chapter Ten

A room, a blue room, decorated lavishly in silver and gold. Soft mattress under her back, pillows in a fluffy embrace around her neck and shoulders. Embroidered swags of curtains hanging from posts on either side.

And the overwhelming feeling of warmth, of security, of being loved.

The door opened, and suddenly she was conscious of her own bare skin, but before she could move, a figure entered and all discomfort fled.

Him.

The sight of him sent heat straight to her center. He smiled and she groaned, pulling back her knees as he slowly approached the bed, his eyes never leaving hers.

Liam...

A sudden blare of noise, and the dream dissipated.

Tara rolled over and slammed her hand down on top of the alarm clock, cursing under her breath. Looking up, she saw that Kiki was also stirring, bleary-eyed and looking disgruntled.

"Is there a reason I had to be up this early?"

"Azure invited me swimming after breakfast. Both of us, actually." Tara threw Kiki an apologetic look, inwardly hoping that she hadn't been moaning in her sleep. *God, that would have been embarrassing.*

With a dramatic eye roll, Kiki threw herself back onto the bed, covering her face.

* * * *

The lack of sleep and hangover still seemed to be affecting her after breakfast. Tara stood in front of the mirror, tying a pale blue sarong over a matching one-piece swimsuit. She tried to ignore the noises behind her as Kiki's bikini-clad reflection flung itself listlessly back and forth, hanging its head forward and shaking it as she let out a groan of exaggerated pain.

Much more of this and she would be forced to wring Kiki's neck.

"Look, can't you just take an aspirin or something?"

"I've already —"

Kiki's retort was cut off by a sharp knock on the door. Tara crossed to open it, holding her breath.

Will it just be her? Or will he — ?

It was both of them.

Azure was a vision in red, bust and hips accentuated by a string bikini and knee-length sarong. Her hair was pulled back in a French plait, exposing a tanned neck and shoulders that left Tara briefly conscious of her own paler skin as she forced her eyes to remain on her sister, fighting to keep them from straying toward the figure behind her.

She hadn't been ready for the sight of Liam Wilder in nothing but swimming shorts.

"Ready?" Azure's voice was cool, and Tara had the immediate feeling of having her mind read.

"Absolutely."

"Good. Grab a towel and let's go."

Tara threw her beach towel over one shoulder, picked up her bag and followed Azure out, Kiki close behind her.

The moment they reached the stern of the boat, Azure dropped bag, towel and sarong against the rail then ran down the steps to the diving platform. With no apparent hesitation she flung herself off the end, her body forming a perfect diver's pose before slicing through the water with barely a splash.

"Christ," Kiki murmured behind Tara. "I'm not diving off that."

"Oh, come on," Tara couldn't resist teasing. "It's easy."

Liam had already reached the platform. He paused on the edge, arms stretched out to the sides, then with a half dreamy, half crazy expression on his face he twirled on the spot and fell backwards, before straightening out just in time to hit the water perfectly.

Tara couldn't draw her eyes away. That was *him*, the Liam she remembered from his adverts. The Liam who had been hers — once.

"Oh, it's easy, is it?" Kiki whispered mockingly from behind her.

Tara forced herself back to reality.

"Of course. Look." She scampered down the steps, threw her arms up and dove, feeling the air rush in her ears before water enveloped her in cold silence. As she surfaced, a sparkling wave slapped her in the face.

"Yay!" Azure's voice came from her left. Shaking the water from her eyes, Tara could see Kiki's head in the center of circular ripples, presumably the result of a dive-bomb.

"You should get her back for that," Liam called out. "Go dunk her, Tara."

Yes!

Kiki's eyes widened. "Don't you dare!"

Galvanized, Tara surged forward. Kiki made a valiant attempt to swim away, but her rather limp breaststroke was no match for Tara's crawl. Kiki let out an outraged yelp as her head and shoulders disappeared underwater.

"Oh, you wait!"

Tara darted out of the way of Kiki's next splash, which hit Azure—Azure responded with interest, and the splash fight was on.

It was quite strange to see Liam Wilder being so...well, wild. His persona had been one of controlled insanity—soft and inviting, then frenetic and explosive. Here, as Tara ducked one arc of water after another and fired her own back, he seemed relaxed, carefree. The contrast made her brain hurt.

And yet, just being near him was *so good...*

"Hey, you guys!"

A figure had appeared at the railings, waving.

Oh God. It was Reese. At the sight of him, every warm feeling fled from Tara's body.

"Hey, Reese!" Azure shouted back. "Come on in!"

Reese ran down to the platform, pinched his nose then leaped into the air, legs flailing in all directions. Tara closed her eyes and winced as he hit the water with a painful-sounding smack.

"Oof," Kiki commented. "That's got to hurt."

"Idiot," Tara muttered.

Reese was swimming toward her, close enough to have heard, but her voice had been drowned by a shout from Liam, who was beginning a sidestroke toward the port side of the yacht.

"Oh, Reese? Look after the ladies for me. It's time for my lap."

"No problem!" Reese shouted back, raising one hand in a thumbs-up as Liam turned to swim away.

Treading water, Reese slowly spun to face Tara, who was becoming uncomfortably aware that Kiki had moved farther away, winking over her shoulder, obviously with the intention of leaving them alone.

"You know," Reese said in a low voice, leaning closer, "you're beautiful when you're wet."

Oh, for fuck's sake. Tara dragged her eyes away from Liam's retreating form and struggled to hide her disdain.

"Yeah. Thanks."

Reese recoiled at her tone.

"What's your problem?"

Tara sighed. "Look. It was great, but it was one time only. I don't do second dates."

From the incredulous expression on Reese's face, it was going to be difficult for him to grasp.

"It's funny," Kiki commented as she floated on her back alongside Azure. "I wouldn't have thought he was her type."

Azure kicked one foot, propelling herself to within arm's reach of the ledge that ran along the base of the stern. "She doesn't really have a type. He's a man."

In fact it didn't look as though there was anything between Reese and Tara at all. Certainly nothing affectionate, anyway.

Reese was gesturing with one arm as he spoke, his movements jerky—every so often he would lose his rhythm and dip under the water before coming back up with a splutter. Tara's jaw was set defensively, her face a cold mask. When Reese paused for breath, Tara spoke, but briefly, and clearly not to Reese's liking.

Azure rolled her eyes and turned back to Kiki, who was pulling herself up to sit on the ledge.

"So how are things going with you know who?"

Kiki froze for a moment then assumed a casual air. "Who?"

"Give it a rest. I'm not dense."

Kiki gave Azure a long, pensive look before apparently deciding that it was pointless. "Fine. As you'd expect, anyway. How did you know?"

"Let's not talk about that, shall we?" Azure raised her eyebrows in warning. "I'm not going to tell anyone else."

Well, it was true enough. Kiki was her friend — Azure would keep her secrets.

And Liam was her husband, and anything learned from him would be her secret too.

The argument between Tara and Reese seemed to be reaching a peak. Tara looked to be torn between defending herself and concealing their discussion — Reese looked to be losing his marbles. Recognizing the dynamic, Azure mentally re-cataloged their relationship as 'former one-night-stands' and watched them out of the corner of her eye.

"Will you *shut up* and keep your voice down?" Tara hissed.

Reese scowled, but lowered his voice. "I think I've got a right to be angry. You *used* me—"

"Oh, please. It was a one-night stand. Don't act like it never happens."

"Yes, and how many women complain about that?"

"Look," Tara snapped. "If I'd wanted a relationship I'd have made you wait. It was fun for both of us. That's it."

God save me from clingy men. Why did he have to be difficult?

Shit, I hope Liam doesn't come back and see this. I'll look like a total whore.

"Fun? It—" Reese, still treading water, gestured again with his arm and lost his balance. Falling sideways, his head plunged underwater mid-rant, leaving him spluttering as he re-surfaced. Tara covered her mouth, but was unable to hide an undignified snort of laughter.

His face stilling, Reese stared at her for an incredulous moment.

"This is all a joke to you, isn't it?"

Tara gave him a long, appraising look.

I'm sick of this. It's not worth it.

"No, it's not a joke. It was fun. Nothing more. If you saw it as more, I'm sorry, but it's not my problem."

In silence they exchanged stares, Reese wide-eyed and disbelieving, Tara challenging. It was Reese who broke first, shaking his head.

"You're a stone cold bitch."

With that, he turned and swam back to the ledge, ignoring Azure and Kiki as he hauled himself out of the water and started up the stairs. Tara deliberately turned away, but found the other two women watching her curiously.

"Everything okay?" Azure asked.

Tara shrugged. "Men."

Azure nodded sympathetically and pushed off the ledge, taking Kiki's foot with her. The ensuing shriek and splash was enough to break the tension left by Reese's departure and Tara joined in the water fight that followed, mentally giving thanks that Liam had been absent.

The last thing she wanted was for him to see her as a slut.

Although, a discomfiting voice reminded her, if he ever remembered their meeting, that horse had bolted already.

"I'm starving."

Catching the beach ball Kiki had just thrown at her, Tara glanced over her shoulder and steeled herself for the sight. Azure was floating dreamily in Liam's arms a few feet away, Liam drifting them both around in lazy circles.

"Yeah, me too," Kiki agreed. "It's got to be nearly lunchtime."

"I thought you were hungover?" Tara tossed the beach ball at her, which bounced off Kiki's head.

Kiki threw it back carelessly. "I was. Now I want lunch."

"Let's get lunch then," Azure suggested without moving. Tara raised an eyebrow.

Is she expecting someone to get it for her or what?

Before she could comment, she realized that Liam's aimless circling was now aimed toward the yacht, while Azure lay back and allowed herself to be towed. As they reached the ledge, Liam climbed up onto it first before crouching down and lifting Azure out of the water, leaving her sitting on the edge.

Interesting.

Tara propelled herself forward, covering the distance to the yacht in four strokes as Kiki trailed behind her. Liam had already disappeared up the steps with Azure behind him. As Tara arrived at the top, she saw Azure drying herself off with a beach towel while Liam was laying another out on one of the sun-loungers.

"You coming for lunch?"

"Nah." Azure sat down on the sun-lounger and dug around in her bag, bringing out a tube of suntan cream. "Liam's going to bring some out here."

Tara blinked. The idea of sitting and waiting for a man—even Liam Wilder—to go and get her some lunch struck her as ridiculous.

Does she have servants to do all this at home, or what? Does he feed her as well?

An image of Liam hand-feeding an indolent, blissful Azure sprang into her mind, bringing with it a wave of nausea that nearly brought Tara to her knees. Oh God, she was not going to watch that. Not now, not ever.

"Okay. I need to get out of the sun before I burn, so—"

"Oh, yeah, of course." Azure was still digging in her bag. As Tara watched, she pulled out a bottle of Evian water and what looked like a small bottle of pills. The label was too small to read, but bore the tiny type and logo of a medical prescription.

She bit her tongue to stop herself asking. If Azure wanted her to know, she would have told her—and she was no longer close enough to hear these things automatically.

But then Azure was taking them right in front of her, and—

One pill, two pills, and Azure tipped her head back to wash them down with water. As she swallowed, she caught Tara's eye and with a sardonically raised eyebrow tapped the side of her nose with one finger.

'Keep your nose out.' Right. Got it. Best to just leave.

"I'll see you later then." *Something polite.* "It was…fun." *Oh, pathetic.*

"Yes." Azure looked up, suncream in hand, and smiled. "It was."

And, with nothing more to say, Tara picked up her towel and bag and left.

* * * *

Twenty minutes later, Tara sat at a round table on the upper deck, panini and chips in front of her, as she idly twirled her fork and stared into space.

It had been easier than she had expected.

Azure had been relaxed. So had he. It had been strange to see him that way — so unaffected, so…*normal.*

So few flashes of the man she knew in her head.

But then, that was the point, wasn't it? To get to know him as a real person. As a man.

At the word 'man', she caught her breath as the memory of her dream filled her mind. Liam had been wearing nothing but shorts today, so close to the shamelessly naked vision of her dreams…

Damn it. I can't do this. I shouldn't do this.

But somewhere in the back of her mind Kiki's words still echoed — *'He's the one breaking his vows, not me. If he loved his wife…'*

Behind her she heard the swing door slap closed. Turning, she saw Ryan approaching, a lazy smile on his face. Tara treated him to her best smile in return, thankful for the distraction.

Ryan was hot. He would do for the time being.

She mentally pushed aside the memory of Reese's angry words — *stone cold bitch* — as Ryan, waving at the waiter, joined her at her table.

Chapter Eleven

Sunlight washed over the lower deck, bathing the stern in a wave of heat. After placing her bottle of suncream on the floor, Tara slipped on her sunglasses and stretched out on the lounger, closing her eyes.

It had been a week. Three days on the Costa Brava, after which the yacht had set sail for Italy. After days of nothing but open water, the Amalfi Coast was coming into view — pretty candy-colored houses climbing the cliffs, somehow both neat and rugged at the same time. Occasionally a car or bus could be seen wending its way along the roads that curved along the cliff edge, climbing in a series of hairpin bends carved into the rock.

Even the days of sailing had been stunning. She had never seen so much sun and sea in her life, so much sparkling water and dancing waves. At one point on the Spanish coast they had watched for dolphins and whales, and while none had breached as dramatically as Tara would have liked, the sight of them cresting in the water had been breathtaking.

The sun was working its magic on everyone. Tara's skin had turned a golden brown, natural blonde highlights forming in her hair. As if to remind everyone that they were twins, Azure was mirroring her, her hair now streaked almost blue, framing an olive-toned face. She wore beachwear constantly, bikinis and sarongs in crimson or sky-blue, diamond-encrusted sunglasses and jeweled pedicures.

Today Tara had chosen her favorite green swimsuit. It complimented her eyes and hair perfectly — not that there was anyone here to see it.

Finding the time to be alone had been surprisingly simple. Kiki had been easy to lose — she was constantly slipping away to see her mystery man. Ryan, she gathered, was in the gym, doing his afternoon workout. Regan had talked her into sharing a plate of deli meat at lunch, but had disappeared to the salon afterwards for a facial. The sun had played havoc with her skin — while her face was one of the few places not burnt, it was dry and flaking, a fact that Regan had bemoaned over and over.

And Azure had gone out in the tender with Liam.

Oh, Liam.

Since their morning swim she had seen him every day. Lunch twice. A trip out to Lloret de Mar in the tender, where Tara had been ready to play bodyguard if necessary. Drinks after dinner, the haze of alcohol and talking, talking, always talking.

She had always wanted him to talk to her, spend time with her, and yet it wasn't enough. It wasn't *right.*

Because he wasn't *hers.*

Liam was always caring, always solicitous. He was always the one to order food, though Azure made her own choices. He was always the one to get the drinks.

Sitting next to Azure, he would always have his arm around her, pillowing Azure's head on his shoulder, stroking her hair. Massaging her shoulders when he apparently thought no one was looking.

He was sweet, he was playful — he was nothing like she had imagined, nothing like his public persona. Where the Liam Wilder she knew from TV had dazzled, he merely glowed. Instead of unpredictable and fiery, he was peaceful, yet teasing.

And the things he would say, and the things Azure said back, were a constant resource of torment.

"Remember that little cocktail bar on the beach in Mexico?"

Or — "It's good, but no one makes this soup like Mrs Porter."

Or, worse still — "No, that was the night I ripped the curtains off the bed."

And Tara would retreat behind her mask while Liam and Azure chatted and laughed, sometimes about experiences shared with other people there, sometimes ones that were just theirs. They would leave the bar behind them later as they walked with arms around each other's waist, whispering, disappearing into their gilded bubble.

It would have been unbearable, except —

Except for one thing.

One evening three nights ago, Azure had excused herself to go to the bathroom just as Kiki and Regan had gone to the bar, leaving Tara alone with Liam. Before she had had time to struggle for conversation, he had spoken.

"Tara, I wanted to ask you something."

Tara's heart had given a painful thump.

Has he finally remembered me?

Has Azure told him how I feel?

Has he guessed?

"When we go out to Lloret tomorrow, I was hoping you could keep an eye on Azure. We should be safe this time, but..." His eyes met hers in sad resignation. "You know what happened last time."

She had swallowed a lump in her throat. "Of course."

"I know you have training for this kind of thing. I hate to ask you to play bodyguard, but—"

"Yes," Tara had broken in. "I'd be happy to."

Liam had smiled, that soft, glowing smile that had drawn her to him in his commercials.

"Thank you. It really means a lot to me."

And for a moment, Tara had looked in his eyes and seen...*something.*

It had been there, she was sure of it, and it had left her breathless and thrilled all evening until she had been able to slip back to her cabin and pleasure herself under the bedcovers.

And it was so different now from before, when she had only known him from TV and that one meet and greet.

* * * *

Four years ago

Azure was deployed, but Tara was on leave. The opportunity had arisen—the meet and greet advertised—and Tara had bought a ticket, joining a group of seven people.

Liam was in character. He moved along the line, shook her hand. They exchanged smiles, and the twenty-two-year-old Tara found herself flushed with desire.

If she had worshiped him before, that was nothing compared to this. Before, it had been a childish passion. Now, as a full-grown adult, just the touch of his hand had her aching for him.

She was so star-struck she temporarily lost all reason. After the meet and greet session, Liam and his crew disappeared into one of the theme park bars, and a small part of Tara urged her to follow.

She did.

The details grew blurred at that point, smeared by alcohol and high spirits. Somehow, drink in hand, she insinuated herself into his group, found herself standing next to him, talking to everyone, but casting sidelong glances in his direction all the time.

Then one of the crewmen excused himself, leading another girl out of the bar to the stairwell, and Tara threw Liam an inviting smile — and the next thing she knew, she was being led upstairs herself to one of the bedrooms on the top floor.

The disappointment she had felt seemed as though it would never end.

It had been so...*impersonal*. They had barely even spoken. Certainly no clothes had come off. She remembered clinging to the post of the four-poster bed, her cheek pressed to the carved wood, jolting with every thrust of the cock inside her and thinking that it could have been anyone back there.

She was no stranger to one-night stands. She had offered, he had taken. No one was to blame. But it hadn't been what she'd had in mind.

She had wanted to feel special, and instead she had felt like a groupie.

There had been no point dragging it out. After it was over, she had rearranged her knickers and skirt and quietly left. As she had passed through the bar, she had seen Liam rejoin the group, public face still on as though nothing had happened.

She hadn't even given him her name.

* * * *

And, disappointing as it was, it had been reasonable at the time, because Liam had still been a world away. She had known it was impossible, it was a dream that would never come true, and she would never even attempt to make it come true. But she had always remembered the touch of his hand, his voice in her ear — it had taken on a new light as it faded into memory, somehow seeming more special than it had been in reality. She had let herself dwell on it, knowing it was silly, but also knowing it didn't matter, because she would never be a part of his world. Never have to face him again.

Until one day it was there, impossible to ignore, because suddenly he was her brother-in-law, and the rejection was palpable. To know that Azure had pierced that world, had achieved what she hadn't...

And he didn't even remember who she was!

The frustration was overwhelming, and could only be relieved by her picturing that moment in the ship's bar, that look in his eyes as her fingers brought her to climax.

Then there was Ryan.

Ryan was less of an annoyance to be around than she had expected. He was an interesting dinner conversationalist when he wasn't twisting every comment into a double entendre. Tara had begun to look forward to the evenings when Kiki was off doing whatever she was doing, although she had begun to wonder how Ryan's roommate felt about being left on his own for dinner.

Another source of wonder was Ryan's opinion of Kiki.

"Alone again, I see?" he had commented dryly a few nights ago, looking over Tara's shoulder to read her menu. "And where's madam this time?"

"Don't know," Tara had answered absently, her attention drawn by the presence of oyster pie on the list of mains. "I'm getting used to it."

Ryan had held his tongue, but Tara hadn't missed the expression of distaste he'd worn as he'd sat down opposite her, and two glasses of wine had persuaded her to ask about it.

"Don't you like Kiki?"

Ryan had raised his eyebrows and taken a bite of his chicken supreme.

"I take it that's a no."

"Let's just say," Ryan had said after a judicious pause, twisting his fork between his fingers, "that I don't like how she acts."

"And what does that mean?"

"Exactly what I said. Take it or leave it." One eyebrow had arched sardonically. "I'm a man. No need to look for hidden meanings in what *I* say."

Tara had glared, and the ensuing heated discussion had prevented any further mention of Kiki.

When he wasn't picking at her roommate, Ryan made an entertaining companion. He seemed to know all the right questions to ignite a conversation, even if he did seem to enjoy poking the fire occasionally.

"So how come you joined the Army?" he had asked one evening over his soup.

Tara had shrugged. "It's in the family. I never wanted to do anything else."

Ryan had asked about Izzie and Roger, whom Tara had been happy to talk about, before asking the ultimate question.

"So why did Azure join?"

"Like I said. It's in the family."

"Yeah, but she was keen enough to quit as soon as she met Liam. *You* said you'd never quit for marriage."

"Well—"

There had been an uncomfortable pause as Tara had untangled her thoughts, in particular one little voice that was wondering if she would have quit for Liam.

She knew the answer, but had never said it out loud.

"Our dad wanted it for all of us. She didn't have much choice."

Ryan had nodded slowly, and Tara had found herself rushing on ahead.

"I thought she liked it too. I didn't—I didn't realize."

It was the truth, and yet guilt stirred in her gut. She should have realized, but she had never asked. In their family, joining the military was simply what was done. Roger had gone first, had joined the Royal Electrical and Mechanical Engineers, and progressed at a rapid rate. Izzie's enthusiasm had been infectious—she would have been happy to go straight in had their father not insisted on Sandhurst, and now she was an officer in Signals. Tara had never questioned the status quo—she had been happy to go along with her father's wishes.

And Azure… Well. Tara did remember arguments, her father shouting and her other the peacemaker. She remembered Azure's suggestion of the RAF as a compromise—one that had gone down like a lead balloon. She remembered Azure finally going with Tara to officer training and joining the Air Corps, and had accepted it as normal—but now it occurred to her that maybe Azure had simply chosen the option that had allowed her to escape.

The fact that it had been the Air Corps had made it more likely, in her mind, that Azure was happy in her career. She had always said she wanted to fly. Tara had envisaged her as a helicopter pilot, maybe even taking Apache training. Loving the Army, as she did herself.

The memory of Azure lying on the sofa had re-emerged, and Tara had briefly wondered if Ryan knew about that before dismissing it. He had said Azure had quit—clearly he didn't know that she had been discharged.

And Liam would be discreet—assuming that Azure had told him.

Oh, Liam.

Ryan was hot. There was no denying that. But when she was in his arms, in her head it was always Liam.

Well, it wasn't as though she was using him that badly. They hadn't had sex. Hell, this was about as near to a relationship as she ever got. A week, and all they'd done was kiss and caress on the deck.

Give it another week and maybe she'd allow him something more. But it wouldn't kill him if she made him wait.

And in the meantime, she could kiss him, press against him, let him touch her and stroke her through her clothes until her body was ready to explode—then say goodnight, slip back to the cabin and finish herself off.

And it would always be Liam her mind screamed, never Ryan.

* * * *

"God, it is *roasting* out there."

Stepping into the cabin, Azure felt the air conditioning hit her body and gave a sigh of relief. Sun was great, but the weather today had been scorching. She kicked off her sandals and crossed to the mirror as Liam disappeared into the bathroom.

"Can you throw me the after-sun while you're in there?" She peeled off her T-shirt and dropped it on the floor, screwing up her face in distaste at the bright red lines at her neck and upper arms. "Ugh. I've definitely burnt."

Liam came out of the bathroom and stood behind Azure, a bottle of lotion in his hand. He squeezed some into his palm and began to apply it to Azure's right arm, his hand gliding over her skin in smooth, even strokes.

Their eyes met in the mirror as his breath skated over the nape of her neck, stirring her hair. Holding his gaze, Azure held out her other arm for him to coat with after-sun.

"Does that hurt?"

"No."

He ran his slick hand up her shoulder, slid her bra strap down and began to stroke first at the base of her neck, then glided it lower, lower, lower, feeling the rise and fall as her breath quickened. Azure's eyes fell closed in pleasure.

"Do you remember this?"

Azure struggled to open her eyes.

"That first night together."

"Yes." A soft kiss to her neck, and Azure moaned. "Four days after you arrived."

"Two days after you moved me out of the guest wing."

"And I walked in on you getting dressed for dinner."

"Yes." Azure let her head fall back onto his shoulder as he slid his hand into the cup of her bra and caressed her breast.

It had been so fast, and yet at the time she had barely noticed. From the first day of meeting him they had been unable to stop talking, unwilling to part in the evening. They had eaten dinner together in the mansion dining room, had had breakfast together the next morning, toured the park together, ridden the rollercoasters—on at least one occasion, holding hands.

By the end of the weekend Liam's publicist had been primed with stories for the press—Liam had asked *'Will you stay the week?'* and Azure had answered *'Yes.'* And by then it had seemed only natural to have her moved from the distant wing into a room in Liam's living quarters.

She had dreamt about him every night. The new bedroom smelled of Liam's aftershave, sending her into a tailspin, and that first night she had been unable to resist touching herself to thoughts of him. She had pictured him slowly undressing her, sliding each item of clothing from her body with teasing touches as she forced herself to stand still, letting him expose her inch by inch.

She'd visualized standing naked before him, letting him worship her body with kisses and licks, caressing her breasts into tingling, peaked sensation, parting her lower folds to explore her with his tongue and probe with his fingers. Then laying her out on the bed, sliding his hard cock inside her then them moving together, again and again, in a rhythm too good to ever end.

She had brought herself to three climaxes that first night alone.

Then that night, when Liam had gone to dress for dinner and left her with a kiss, she had dressed herself with more care than usual.

She had deliberately taken her time. Deliberately chosen a chiffon dress that required a second layer, so that when Liam had opened the door she had been standing in front of the mirror in nothing but a silk slip.

He had concealed it well, but she had seen the desire on his face, as well as the tension in his body that spoke of his thoughts of apologizing and leaving her to it.

"Could you help me with my necklace? I can't fasten it." It was an excuse, of course, although her hands were trembling. *I want you, Liam – I want you so much.*

Liam had closed the door and crossed to stand behind her. He had taken the silver necklace from her and laid it around her neck as she lifted her hair in a silky arc.

Then, as now, his breath had stirred her hair, but then his fingers had shaken just a little as he'd handled the clasp, and Azure had thrilled at the thought that he had been just as affected as she was.

"You don't mind, do you?"

"Mind?"

"That I'm not dressed yet?" Azure had asked archly. "It doesn't bother you?"

Liam had paused for a moment, and the tension between them had filled the air.

"That depends what you mean by *bother.*"

Azure had let her hair fall to her shoulders. Liam had caught it and pushed it to the side, exposing the curve of her neck.

"You've never seen me like this before. I thought you might—" Her words had turned into a gasp as Liam had leaned in to kiss below her ear.

"Thought I might what?" His kisses had trailed farther down her neck, removing all capacity for thought.

"I don't know."

Her breath had come faster, and Liam had placed his hands on her shoulders, softly massaging as he'd lifted his mouth from her neck.

"I didn't expect—" Liam had broken off as Azure had raised her left arm, curving it behind her to hook over his shoulder, and he'd kissed her as she'd turned her face to him.

"What?"

"I didn't expect to want you this much. Oh God, tell me to stop."

And his mouth had been back on hers, his hands cupping her breasts, and Azure's last thought had been, *Never, never stop.*

Now, as she opened her eyes to watch Liam and her in the mirror, Liam had unfastened her bra and was caressing her breasts in that same way, still kissing her neck, and Azure felt a sudden urge for his mouth in more important places.

As she opened her mouth to speak, he softly tweaked a nipple. She cried out, pushing her hips back against his body—his hardness pressed against her bottom and Liam groaned. "*Now.*"

"*Yes.*"

The bed was just a few feet behind them. They stumbled toward it, still kissing, their clothes strewn over the floor until they fell, both naked, onto the silken duvet. Azure rolled onto her side and slid down the bed until she was in line with Liam's hips, reaching out to grip his cock and take it into her mouth.

Liam groaned and pushed forward. Azure held him tightly at the base and slid him farther in, inch by inch until her mouth met her fingers, then drew back, gliding her lips over the sensitive skin as she dragged her tongue along the underside.

Another groan, and she felt Liam's hands lace into her hair and tug — she knew what he wanted, and pulling away, she pushed herself along the bed until she was on the pillows. Azure stretched her arms above her head and gripped the headboard, arching her back as Liam buried his face between her breasts before trailing long, slow kisses down her body to her pussy.

"*Oh!*"

He always knew how to do this, how to drive her insane with every slow glide of his tongue, and she moaned in pleasure as her toes curled and her inner muscles clenched, wanting him — *wanting him* — inside but not wanting him to stop, not yet, not yet —

"Liam..."

And Liam was on her, and their mouths met again as he slid inside her in one long thrust.

Azure let her arms fall around him and held on as their bodies rocked together, first slowly, then faster as the heat increased. Her fingers tightened on his shoulders as the first tinglings of pleasure began — they were gasping, shaking, slick with sweat as their motion built into a frenzy and Azure let out a desperate cry just as Liam dropped his face to her neck, moaning something...

Then the pleasure hit her, and her body convulsed around him. Liam groaned and collapsed on top of her.

* * * *

The morning sun had been pleasant, but the midday sun was suffocating. Tara carefully packed her belongings back into her bag and made her way down to the main deck. Hopefully Kiki would be out of their room so she could change and go for some lunch.

The deck was mostly deserted, although Tara could make out the figures of a middle-aged couple at the bow. The breeze down here was refreshing, and she paused to lean over the railing, allowing the air to whip her hair into a golden flurry.

As she stood, watching the Amalfi Coast as it bobbed in the distance, the yacht hit a wave, showering her with a cooling spray. God, that was better. Her skin had been on fire up there.

Lost in enjoyment, she barely heard it, but a faint sound carried by the wind caught her ear.

Was that…?

Turning, she scanned the numbers on the nearby doors, and realized that she was close to Azure's cabin.

Azure and Liam's cabin.

Another cry, and although some part of her *knew*, she found herself moving inexorably forward until she was outside the porthole that looked into their cabin.

She had known, and yet the reality was a stab to the gut.

Azure was lying back on the bed, blue-black hair in a wash across the pillow. Her body was half concealed, showing only a long, glistening flank extending from head to toe. Concealed because she was locked in a passionate embrace with the man Tara had known from TV and photographs, watched, dreamt of, and only now she found herself admitting the truth.

I'm in love with him.

And she had never seen him naked before — and it was a stab, as she remembered that he had never taken his clothes off during their encounter — but he was there, *right there*, his body smooth, light reflecting from curved muscles and the twin rises of his buttocks. His arms were locked around Azure's neck, his hips slowly, torturously thrusting between hers. And though their faces were unclear in the glass she could see that they were kissing, kissing as their movements increased and Azure's voice was rising in a moan —

Frozen for a moment, numbness giving way to horror, Tara viciously pushed herself away from the cabin wall and ran.

Her room was empty. Kicking the door shut behind her, she fell into the bathroom and collapsed over the toilet just before she was violently sick.

Oh God. Oh God. Oh God.

It was a nightmare. And she was trapped here with them — she had nowhere to go.

I should never have come. I can't get away.

The image of them kissing was indelible in her mind. She remembered Reese, their cold and unemotional sex compared with Azure and Liam making love, *making love*, and Reese's words echoed again in her head — *'You're a stone cold bitch.'*

But Ryan didn't think she was cold.

Ryan.

There was nowhere else to go. No one else to take this feeling from her.

She slowly stood, unsteadily, and looked at herself in the mirror. Her hair was windblown — in her mind she re-categorized it as 'sexily rumpled'. Her makeup was still intact, with a slight smudginess around the eyes that gave them a smoky look. Her mouth was still reddened, but felt disgusting. She reached for the mouthwash, swirled, spat.

Ryan. Think of Ryan.

She stared at herself in the mirror, eyelashes lowered, as she practiced expressions with her lips, until she was satisfied with the image that looked back. Reaching behind herself, she unfastened her bikini and sarong and let them drop, leaving them on the bathroom floor as she walked into the bedroom.

Red lace underwear. Red vest top. Long red skirt in a floating fabric. Sandals. That should do it.

Fifteen minutes later, dressed head to toe in crimson, Tara left the cabin, locking the door behind her. Ryan should be back from the gym by now.

His roommate had better be out, she thought as she crossed the deck with determined paces.

Because if not, I'm throwing him out, and if he won't go, he's getting a show.

Chapter Twelve

The dim sound of a Savage Garden track could be heard through Ryan's bedroom door when Tara arrived.

Obviously somebody was in, at any rate. She knocked.

"It's open," Ryan called from inside.

Good. One obstacle down.

Tara opened the door and leaned through it. Ryan was lying on the nearest bed, arms folded behind his head, wearing nothing but a pair of blue and white board shorts. Tara raised an appraising eyebrow, letting her eyes glide down his tanned, muscular chest to the blond trail that ran teasingly under his waistband, resting her gaze finally on the raised bulge beneath the fabric.

Ryan shifted his hips casually, and Tara realized that she had been staring a little too long. She flicked her eyes back to his face, which was wearing a smug smile.

"Hi."

"Hi." Ryan swung his legs over the side of the bed and came over to her. "You eaten yet?"

"Not yet." Tara tipped her head back, offering her mouth for Ryan's kiss. Ryan cupped her chin in his hands and ran his thumb along her lower lip, teasing, before replacing it with his own lips.

He tangled his hands in her hair, grazing her scalp. Tara sighed, opening her mouth wider to let his tongue strafe hers. She could feel his heartbeat already quickening. Pressing herself against the hard length of his body, she let her hands wander down his back and sharply squeezed his buttocks, giggling softly when Ryan jerked in surprise.

"You know…" she breathed in his ear. "Maybe we could go for lunch—after."

Still holding her in his arms, Ryan moved back to look her in the face. Tara involuntarily shivered at the heat in his eyes.

"After?" His voice was ragged.

Tara caught her breath.

"After," she whispered, and moved forward to kiss him again, pushing him backwards at the same time.

The force of her push tumbled them both onto the bed, and Tara immediately straddled his hips, running her hands down his chest—but before she could hook her fingers into the top of his shorts, Ryan caught her wrists in both hands.

What the hell? Automatically Tara tugged against him, but was surprised to find that he had an iron grip. As she raised her head to give him an outraged look, she saw that he was smiling sardonically.

"Uh-uh. I like to be in charge too, Golden Girl."

A sharp yank, and Tara found herself sprawled across his body, Ryan's hands immediately dropping to her hips. He gripped her thigh with one hand and pulled it forward. With the other he pushed her right leg away, causing her to roll sideways. Pressing her hands onto the mattress, she fought to sit up again, but Ryan's hands had moved to her back and held her still.

"Frisky, aren't we? You behave."

And one hand disappeared, only to land with a sharp smack on her bottom.

Oh!

The shock of the moment held Tara still, stunned. Ryan took the opportunity to roll her onto her back and kiss her again, pressing her hands up against the pillow. Tara returned the kiss, even as her mind was spinning and protesting.

He had *spanked* her.

It hadn't been especially hard. The sting was already fading away. No, it wasn't the pain—it was the thought of being spanked, of submitting to his discipline.

And she wanted it. She actually wanted to submit to him.

Tara's spine arched in desire and she moaned into the kiss. Ryan growled in response, letting go of her hands to tangle his own in her hair.

No, damn it! You are not in charge!

She knew she was strong, but not strong enough to roll him off her. Instead, Tara slid her hands down and tugged at his shorts, digging her fingers into his buttocks. Breaking the kiss, Ryan drew himself up on his elbows and looked down at her, his mouth quirked in a half-smile.

"Now that wouldn't be fair, would it?"

Then, without warning, he rolled over onto his back, gripped her arm and tugged, and Tara found herself sprawled across his lap.

"Hey!"

She squirmed, but Ryan had one arm firmly across her shoulders, and Tara found herself securely pinned.

"Hold still, Golden Girl."

And, before Tara could protest, he brought his other hand down on her arse.

Tara gasped in outrage, but to her horror it was more than that—the tingling was spreading from that one spot, sending shock waves to her core, and she bit her lip as she realized what was happening.

He had put her across his knee and was spanking her. And she *liked* it. Worse, the position she was in was both unbearably humiliating and hopelessly exciting, and the suggestion of submission was sending heat to her cunt.

Another swat to her other cheek made her body jolt, and she bit her lip as her cunt grew wetter. *I am not turned on by this. I am not.*

Except she was. And Ryan knew it. In one swift movement he lifted her up and tossed her back onto the mattress. Before Tara could think, he reached downwards and yanked her vest top over her head, taking her unclasped bra with it.

Tara opened her mouth to protest before reconsidering. It would all be coming off eventually, after all. She pushed her skirt and knickers over her hips, letting Ryan strip them the rest of the way down. Before she could sit up, Ryan had caught her shoulders and lowered her back onto the bed.

"Keep still, you."

Damn it, I am not submitting to you!

Before she could argue with him, Ryan had cupped her breasts with both hands and was massaging them, his thumbs stroking her nipples as they hardened under his touch. Tara gasped, her head falling back as a wave of pleasure overwhelmed her.

"That's it," Ryan murmured. "Let it go."

Let it go.

The words struck a chord in her head. She had come to his room ready to take charge as she always did—she never, ever allowed a man to dominate her. And yet here was Ryan, taking control, making her *want* him to take control—making her want to let herself go with him.

It was an unnerving thought.

Ryan's hands moved, his weight shifted, and Tara looked up just as he pushed her thighs apart, settling himself between them. He caught her eye and held it as he used his fingers to idly toy with her folds, an eyebrow arching as he watched for her reaction.

Oh, you bastard. Tara glared down at him, fighting to keep the desire from her face, but God, he was teasing her and he *knew* it, damn him—his fingers were so close to where she wanted them, and her clit was aching for his touch.

"Please." *There, I said it. Happy?*

Ryan threw her a grin before descending upon her, and Tara fell back into the pillow as his tongue began that delicious drag and probe. Two of his fingers slipped inside her, twisting, and Tara bucked against him as he found that spot inside, pulling a deep groan from her.

His fingers weren't enough—she wanted his cock inside her, and God, was that difficult to admit. Forcing herself to move—and stifling a moan at the loss of his tongue—Tara sat up, meeting Ryan's eye firmly as he looked up.

"Fuck me."

Ryan's smile became almost impossibly smug, as if he had just been waiting for her to ask, and he rolled onto his back, his cock hard against his flat stomach. Tara straddled him, lowering herself slowly down onto his shaft until he was inside her to the hilt.

She rose up on her knees, beginning a torturously slow movement up, down, up, watching his face. *Let's see how you like it.* Ryan held her gaze, but the tension was building in his eyes, a crease forming between his eyebrows, and she deliberately kept her motion slow, making him wait.

Then one of Ryan's hands came down hard on one cheek of her bottom.

Tara gasped, startled. *You bastard!* But then the outrage was replaced by hot, urgent lust, and she lost the battle with herself, forced to admit the truth—she couldn't wait another moment.

She had to come, and she had to come *now.*

Leaning forward, she gripped Ryan's arms and squeezed her inner muscles at the same time. Ryan groaned and slammed his hips upwards, his hands tightening on her waist to hold her still as he thrust, over and over. He slid one hand over her thigh to press his thumb to her clit, rotating on the pulsing nub until all her attention was drawn to that one point of pleasure.

"*Ryan!*"

And with that last cry her body clenched down on him as sensation rippled outwards, and Ryan let out a deep moan and collapsed onto the bed, pulling her down on top of him.

* * * *

Afterwards, Tara could barely remember how she had left.

She had made some excuse that Ryan had apparently bought—he had been sleepy, probably too sleepy to argue. Or maybe he had seen through the brittle mask of composure she had thrown on in a desperate attempt to get away and sort out her head.

She had wanted him to take her mind off Azure and Liam—and he had done that, although the images still floated through her mind, making her heart twist. But more, he had made her want him. Want him to dominate her. Want him to *spank* her.

It was wrong. It was just *wrong.*

And—afterwards, before she had found a reason to leave, she had collapsed on top of him, his arms had folded round her and somehow they had been cuddling. *Cuddling!*

She never cuddled. Hell, she rarely stayed on the bed for more than five minutes afterwards. Yet she had found herself wanting to stay wrapped in his arms, enveloped in that warm, comforting cocoon.

Of course, she had been upset from earlier. That must have been it. She had needed the comfort. But still, his tender caresses, soft whispers in her ear—it wasn't what she was used to, and his affection lingered on her body.

To think of letting him touch her again— *No.* Her mind refused even as her body rebelled against the thought.

I won't let him do this to me. I won't.

But a small part of her whispered that she would.

Chapter Thirteen

The first thing Tara noticed at dinner was the bottle of champagne on the table.

The second thing was the presence of Kiki.

"Not meeting the mystery man tonight?"

Kiki threw her a sardonic look.

"No. So Ryan will just have to sit at his own table tonight."

"I think he'll survive." Tara sat down and picked up the menu, deliberately keeping her mask on. Dinner with Ryan had loomed like a nightmare, but she was damned if she would let Kiki know.

The thought of Ryan sitting across from her, watching her with those knowing eyes, made her stomach clench. She had wanted only one thing from him — a distraction from the reality of Azure's marriage. And yet somehow it had gone so differently.

She had *wanted* him.

Hell, she had wanted to *submit* to him.

It was wrong, it was stupid, it was completely the opposite of what she had intended. And yet her mind was all over the place and her body still felt imprinted by his touch.

"Wonder what the champagne's for," she commented casually.

Kiki gave a half-hearted shrug and fixed her eyes on her menu, every inch of her tense figure radiating waves of *do not talk.*

Ugh. So it was to be a silent dinner as opposed to a tumultuous dinner. Tara wasn't sure which was worse.

As they were finishing off their starters, the clinking of fork against glass cut through the air. Putting down a forkful of scallop, Tara twisted in her seat as all other heads turned in a wave of movement, ending in the figure of Nik Sugiyama, who was standing up in his seat with a glass of champagne in his hand. Beside her, she was vaguely aware of a waiter appearing and picking up the bottle on their table.

"Thank you, ladies and gentlemen. I have an announcement to make."

Around the room Tara could hear the muted pop of corks, followed by the slosh and fizz of glasses being filled. Obviously they were about to have a toast.

"Tonight is a very special occasion for us," Nik continued, glancing down at Tracey, who was smiling up at him from her seat. "Because tonight I am very happy to announce that my wonderful wife and I are expecting our first child."

A ripple of delighted noises ran around the room— somewhere to Tara's right clapping began and Tara joined in, automatically glancing across the room toward Liam's table. Liam was on his feet, applauding enthusiastically, but Tara saw him pause to cast a glance down at Azure, resting one hand protectively on her shoulder.

Quickly Tara looked away, focusing on Nik, who was now raising his glass.

"Thank you. Thank you. I'd like to propose a toast." He lifted the flute a little higher. "To Tracey."

Tara picked up her newly-filled champagne glass and joined the chorus of voices. "To Tracey!"

"And, to celebrate," Nik continued, "tomorrow night we will be throwing a dinner dance. So everyone has an excuse to wear those ball gowns I know you brought." He sat back down to laughter from around the room.

Tara turned her attention to her food, eyebrows raised. She looked over at Kiki, who was downing her champagne in one gulp.

"Dinner dance, huh?"

"Mmm." Kiki swallowed her mouthful, rolling her eyes at the same time. "How that differs from every other night I don't know."

"Good job I actually brought a ball gown with me." It had been mentioned in the letter that had followed her invitation—*bring evening wear*—but, not knowing exactly what that meant, Tara had brought a range of outfits at varying levels of formality.

"Yeah." Kiki refilled her glass and took another swig. "What fun that's going to be."

Whatever. Tara dismissed Kiki's mood from her mind and refilled her glass. Kiki took the bottle from her as soon as Tara had finished, and poured with a fervor that suggested she would rather be drinking it through a funnel.

So Tracey was pregnant. The image of Liam's hand lingering on Azure's shoulder floated in her mind. Maybe they were trying for a baby too. Her gut clenched at the thought. *Oh God, no.*

She forced herself to be sensible. Azure had always wanted children, she knew. It was more surprising that they hadn't had children already, given that they had been married two years. And—being reasonable—Liam probably wouldn't want to wait a long time. He was twenty years older than Azure. He might even have ideas about bringing up a son to take over the Land of Light business.

But still, the thought of Azure having *his* baby—of trying for a child with him—made her shudder. Automatically her hand went to her stomach. A *baby...*

She needed a distraction.

Ryan.

The memory of their romp still tingled on her skin. As the plates were cleared and the main courses brought, Tara turned her focus inwards and spoke to herself sternly.

So she had enjoyed it. Good. That was what sex was for.

So she had wanted him. Fine.

So she had wanted to submit to him. Not fine. She wouldn't do that again. But they could still have fun, and next time she would show him that she knew how to take charge.

Another image sent a rush of heat to her cunt, making her shift awkwardly in her chair—herself bent over Ryan's lap, submitting to his hand—and she bit down hard on her lip as her hand reflexively clenched on the stem of her glass.

No. Not happening. Never.

And as the meal drew to a close, and Kiki, now hopelessly drunk, stumbled away to their cabin, Tara kept that thought in her mind even as she watched Ryan approach their table.

Even as he drew her into his arms so they could dance.

Even as she succumbed to his kiss.

Even as they burst through his cabin door and fell onto his bed—him above her, taking charge, with no idea that she was *letting* him, letting him think whatever he liked as long as she could take her pleasure.

You will never master me. Never.

* * * *

"Wow. You look amazing."

Tara smiled up at Ryan as he stood by her chair. *Good. That was the idea.*

She cast a glance across the table at Kiki, who was casually leaning back in her seat, ignoring them. If there was one person in the room who had made more effort than herself, it was Kiki. For a full two hours before the dinner dance Kiki had been styling and re-styling her hair, applying makeup with careful shading and highlighting, trying on dress after dress until her bed was buried in silk and velvet. Now, with blonde hair floating around her face, eyes glowing in three shades of green to match her emerald gown, Kiki looked stunning—and like she knew it.

Not that Tara didn't know herself how good she looked. With her blonde coloring she knew she looked spectacular in scarlet, and the dress she had chosen was designed to emphasize every curve, with a slash along the side to expose her leg. The neckline plunged a little lower than she liked—it was more Azure's style—but she had chosen to draw more attention to it with a ruby necklace that dipped into her cleavage.

That should get his attention.

And if the *he* in her head was not the *he* in front of her, nobody would know.

"Are you all right, honey?"

Azure blinked, realizing that she had been staring into space. She looked over at Liam, who was watching her with a concerned look on his face. "Yeah, sorry. Miles away."

"You know, if it's too difficult for you, we can go early."

"No, no, I'm fine. I'm glad she's happy."

Her eyes rested on Tracey, who was talking animatedly to her husband, one hand resting on her still-flat stomach protectively. There were many reasons she could have had for wanting to avoid the woman—a fact of which Liam was fully aware—but her pregnancy wasn't one of them.

However, she knew Liam would find that hard to believe after everything that had happened.

She cast a glance over at Tara and Kiki's table. Both looked like they were dressed to impress—Kiki especially, which was no surprise to Azure. Glittering in green, eyes burning, she looked like a beautiful Lamia. Of course, her rivalry with Tracey would make tonight complicated—no wonder she was ticking all the boxes.

And Tara! Tara had never been ashamed of her body, but she had always preferred to show off her legs rather than her chest, being more straight up and down than Azure. Yet tonight she was a vision in red, her dress low-cut and carefully designed to draw in her waist and flare at her hips, bringing curves and bust where formerly there had been little.

No wonder Ryan's dragging his tongue on the floor.

Azure glanced down at her own gown, silver and one-shouldered, and idly wondered if she should have chosen something lower-cut herself.

Nah. The advantage of D-cups was that she didn't need to show them off. They made themselves known.

She looked up again as a movement caught her attention. Kiki had gotten up and was walking toward Nik and Tracey's table. As Azure watched, Kiki stopped beside Nik and held out her hand — she looked as though she was asking him to dance.

Azure had seen Tracey turn down dances several times already, pleading pregnancy. It was a shrewd move on Kiki's part, guaranteed to make herself look innocent while pissing Tracey off — and from the glare that Tracey was giving her, it was working.

Nik, apparently oblivious to the visual catfight going on around him, took Kiki's hand with a smile and stood, leading her to the dance floor. Azure drew her eyes away, covering her mouth to hide the smile that was already forming.

God, those two.

Tara was also standing, turning to speak to Ryan before gesturing toward Azure's table. *What the hell is she doing?* Ryan glanced over his shoulder, meeting Azure's eye briefly, then said something in response that seemed to suit Tara. She slid past him with a smile and crossed the dance floor toward her.

"Ryan was just about to ask you to dance."

"Oh?" Azure threw a teasing glance at Ryan, who had arrived a step behind. "I didn't know you were sending messengers now."

Ryan winked at her. "Oh, she does everything I tell her."

From the expression that crossed Tara's face, that had *not* been part of the conversation. Before anything more could be said, Azure stood and took the hand Ryan held out, smiling at Tara as she passed her.

"You do realize you're going to suffer for that, don't you?" she commented as they reached the middle of the dance floor.

Ryan arched an eyebrow and smirked.

"I'm looking forward to it."

Sitting in the chair Azure had vacated, Tara watched the pair leave and fought against the urge to grip something, anything, to hide her shaking hands.

She was alone with Liam.

Every over-romanticised cliché she had ever despised seemed to be overwhelming her. Her skin was alive with the sense of his closeness, every hair standing on end. The thought of speaking to him sent her throat into a tight spasm.

Damn it, I am not some trembling twit. I can talk.

It was ridiculously unfair. She just didn't *do* falling in love. This sort of thing should have been over and done with when she was a teenager. Instead here she was, turning into an over-excited fool when all she wanted was to impress him—

Oh God. Impress him? What the hell am I, twelve?

An image of what she really wanted flashed into her mind, and her gut tightened. Herself sprawled on her bed, Liam's arms around her, his cock thrusting inside her, and his voice whispering in her ear, *'It should have been you... It was always you...'*

Stop it. She couldn't sit there in silence. She had to say something—and the only topic of conversation she could think of, damn it, was her sister.

"She looks amazing tonight, doesn't she?"

As Tara spoke, she cast a glance at Liam, who was leaning back in his seat, gazing at the distant figure of Azure with an air of peaceful pleasure.

"She does. She bought that dress specially."

Tara bit her lip. He sounded so...*smitten.*

"It's great to see her so happy. I know our mother was worried it was all too fast."

"I guess she would." Liam shrugged calmly. "It just...worked."

Tara took a sip of champagne to give herself a moment to think. Somehow every possible following sentence seemed rude and intrusive.

You hadn't been married before...

You're a lot older than her...

Could it have 'just worked' with me?

Liam cleared his throat, and Tara took another mouthful as she listened.

"I've never met anyone like her. She's been through so much, and yet she's never lost her spirit. She's one of the strongest people I've ever known."

"She doesn't always look—" *Fuck!* Tara froze, inwardly cursing, but Liam didn't seem offended.

"You can blame me for that, if you like. I've been told I'm over-protective. I guess that's right." He smiled, waving one hand airily in dismissal. "But I think she likes that. It makes her feel safe. And after all that happened..."

Tara held her breath at the expression that crossed Liam's face. All the light had gone, replaced with something...ugly. Something *sickening.*

"I—"

"I know it's old-fashioned," Liam interrupted, as though he hadn't even heard her. "But I will never like the idea of women on the front line."

Tara's stomach churned—coldness flooded her insides and she looked away hastily in case it showed in her face.

It wasn't as though she hadn't heard this opinion before. Women on the front line. Women in the Army at all. There were still plenty of men willing to buy into it, even those in the Army themselves, although much fewer than there had been in the past. But to hear it from Liam Wilder—no. It wasn't right.

He had said *old-fashioned*. Maybe that was true. In a lot of the older men she had heard it from, it had been less real sexism and hostility than a tradition, a need to protect. Not that women *couldn't*, but that they shouldn't have to—an automatic revulsion toward women being threatened, injured, killed.

Or tortured.

"Really?"

She could hear the coolness in her voice. Apparently so could Liam.

"I don't mean to insult you. You're obviously capable. So was Azure. But there are some things—"

Liam's voice cracked. Tara slid her eyes toward him, just in time to see a flash of pain contort his face, his mouth tightening.

"Some—" He cleared his throat. "Some things that should never happen to a woman."

There was something underlying his words, something that made Tara fall very still. She felt she knew what it was—or that she *should* know—but that she still lacked pieces of the puzzle, pieces she might have had if she hadn't cut contact with Azure.

If she had dug deeper, instead of losing patience with the broken figure lying on the sofa, dead-eyed and listless, seeming to buckle under an invisible weight.

"They happen to men too, you know."

Liam paused then turned to face her. He held her gaze for a moment, as if judging her, then gave one firm nod. "I know. And they shouldn't happen to any soldier. But—" He glanced across at the dance floor again, where Azure and Ryan had joined several others in the Macarena. "I look at Azure, I see what it did to her, and all I can think is that *someone did that to my wife*. And I will never be happy that any woman is in that position."

The venom in his voice was almost palpable, and Tara involuntarily recoiled.

Jesus. He had really thought about this. It was more than tradition—it was a visceral reaction.

And one she had encountered before, when men were talking about a daughter, girlfriend, or wife—

Wife!

As the word echoed in her head, she clenched her jaw and closed her eyes, forcing her control back into place. She had known what she was getting into when trying to insinuate herself into Liam's life. But Kiki's casual philosophy toward marriage and affairs seemed to crumble in the face of such protection, such *devotion.*

Silence had fallen again between them. Tara opened her mouth to say something, anything, but was cut off by a short, mirthless laugh from Liam.

"I'm sorry. Rather a dangerous topic for a relaxing evening."

Tara let out a breathless laugh that, to her ears, sounded slightly hysterical.

"Yeah. It's good news for Nik and Tracey, isn't it?"

"Oh, certainly." Liam glanced across the room toward the tables.

Tara, following his gaze, noticed that Tracey was still sitting alone, glass of water in hand and wearing an expression of barely concealed rage. She looked back at Liam and caught a glint of something— humor?—in his eye.

Hmm. Maybe he doesn't like her either.

"Had they been trying long?"

"To be honest, I'm not sure. I've never discussed it with them." There was an odd note to Liam's voice, and a rush of cold—a premonition—hit Tara's gut.

"No, I don't suppose you would."

"No."

Oh God. The humor was gone from Liam's face, replaced by a wistful sorrow, and Tara clenched her fingers around the stem of her glass. *Please don't say it. Please.*

"It's a difficult topic. Well, you know. I'm sure Azure told you about the miscarriages."

Oh shit.

"Of course," Tara managed to get out. "Horrible."

Liam took a long swallow of his champagne, followed by a deep breath. He turned to Tara and smiled, apparently to calm her embarrassment.

"We haven't yet been blessed, but there's time. There's always time."

"Absolutely." Tara forced a smile.

The music was ending, and she could see Azure and Ryan approaching their table. *Thank God.* She couldn't face another second alone with Liam.

She had known Azure had suffered. The details she had left unspoken. She shouldn't have—she could see that now. But she had avoided them, taken the easy way out.

And now this.

Miscarriages.

Her head was in a whirl. One side of her was screaming, *Not that pain, not my sister* and the other cried back, *Not with Liam, not with him* – and above it all, a deeper ache from a memory she had desperately tried to bury…

Ryan was standing in front of her, offering his hand, and Tara took it, wanting something, anything, to steal her thoughts away from what she had heard.

Ryan, Ryan, Ryan.

She had to leave, and she had to leave *now.*

The cabin door banged open as Tara hustled Ryan through it, taking the room in with a brief glance. No sign of the roommate. *Good.*

"Whoa!" Ryan fumbled with the door, struggling to close and lock it as Tara attempted to urge him toward the bed. "You going to start without me?"

Tara choked out a wild laugh and wrestled him backwards until his calves hit the bedframe. Surging forward, she used her full body weight to push him down onto the mattress. She climbed on top of him, kneeling across his thighs, and reached down to unfasten his trousers.

"Hey, Golden Girl." His hand caught her arm.

She looked up to see Ryan watching her with an expression between desire and concern. "You okay?"

No, I'm not okay. I don't know what the hell I'm doing.

For a moment, the urge to give way, to *submit*, was overwhelming. Tara bit her lip, feeling a tremor start somewhere deep inside her body.

No. Tonight she needed to be in control.

Ryan was still looking worried, and Tara flashed him a mischievous smile. "Oh yeah. I just have this major urge to blow you. I hope you don't mind."

Any response Ryan might have given seemed to stick in his throat. Resuming her efforts, Tara dragged the waistbands of his trousers and boxer shorts over his hips, exposing the golden trail of hair that led to his stiff cock.

God, this was one of her favorite things to do. She was already anticipating the dark taste, the silky yet uneven feel on her tongue, hearing the moans and the cries and seeing his balls tightening at that last point of no return. She had done it so often that she had learned to relax her throat, and the ability to take his shaft in to the root would always be appreciated, she found — especially as it left her hands free to roam.

Ryan's cock was perfect — just thick enough to fill her mouth, just long enough to satisfy without making her choke. She would have preferred an uncut foreskin, but what the hell. As she stared down at his cock, at the blond fuzz and the glistening bead of pre-cum at the head, a deep yearning began to grow in her throat.

Oh. His musky scent rose to envelop her, and involuntarily her fingers clenched in his belt loops. Unable to resist, she dropped into a crouch and opened her mouth over his shaft, slowly sliding her lips down, down, down until he hit the back of her throat.

"Fuck—"

The voice was Ryan's, and in her head Tara fought to change it to Liam's. But somehow it hit a wall. *WRONG. WRONG. WRONG.*

Liam...

No. Ryan.

The dark taste of him, edged with the salty flavor of his juices, filled her mouth, and she drew her lips upwards, then back down, back up in a slow, inexorable rhythm. Pressing her hands down on his hips she felt him struggle to thrust. She hummed softly and felt him jolt, his breath escaping in a cry.

That's it. Oh yes.

"Oh God," Ryan moaned, shifting beneath her. "Please…"

Yes, Tara thought as desire twisted in her gut. *I control this. I control you.*

She slid one hand up to cup his balls, feeling them tighten as she caressed him, and his body started to buck against her. He was gasping, groaning, and more of that delicious salty taste was spreading over her tongue — he was close, so close —

"*Oh!*"

Oh, Tara's mind echoed as Ryan cried out, and that familiar taste flooded her throat, her senses overwhelmed with *Ryan, Ryan, Ryan.*

For a long moment, silence fell between them. Tara rested her head on his stomach, feeling his breathing slowing as she savored the feeling running through her body.

The sense of her own power.

Above her, Ryan caught his breath to speak.

"That was —"

I know, Tara thought smugly. *I'm good.*

Before Ryan could finish, the sound of a key in the lock cut across his voice. Immediately Tara leaped backwards, freeing Ryan to hastily drag his trousers back up over his softening cock.

Damn it. She'd forgotten about his roommate.

But then it was probably for the best. She could go back to her own cabin and finish things herself.

"I'll see you tomorrow," she mouthed to Ryan as she crossed to the door, before pressing a kiss to her fingers and waving to him. Ryan, now sitting back against the headboard, flashed her an 'Okay' sign and winked. His trousers were still unbuttoned, but were at least back in place, although she could still glimpse blond fuzz through the gap.

The door opened behind her and Tara darted straight out onto the darkened deck. She had a brief impression of a startled young man and bit back a giggle. *You'd have been even more surprised five minutes earlier.*

The memory sent an ache to her cunt, and she broke into a trot, wanting to get back to her room as soon as possible. Unfulfilled desire was gathering in her gut, impatient to be released.

Maybe this time, she thought as she reached her cabin door, *I'll think about Ryan.*

Chapter Fourteen

Morning found Tara wandering aimlessly around the lower decks of the yacht, doing her best not to be seen.

More than anything, she wanted to be alone. She had managed to avoid Ryan at breakfast by grabbing a slice of toast at full speed and eating it on the run — although since the dining room had been mostly empty, he might still have been in bed. The gym was too dangerous — she knew he went there for early workouts. So she had disappeared into the maze of corridors, hunting for a quiet place to untangle her thoughts.

As she rounded a corner, a familiar doorway presented itself ahead of her.

The chapel.

Tara quickly darted through the door and slid into a seat at the back of the room. Closing her eyes, she rested her head on the back of the chair, letting the silent stillness of the air close in on her.

This was the worst part of being stuck on the yacht. She was surrounded by Ryan, Liam and Azure, and with no way to escape, nowhere to run.

Ryan. God, how her body rebelled at that thought. She had taken charge last night, absolutely — and yet she had still been filled with that overwhelming *want* that she had felt the night he had spanked her arse. Damn it, he had no *right* stirring her up like this. Liam would never have spanked her like that.

Liam. A strange ache made itself known behind her heart as she remembered his words about women on the front line. She had been trying to excuse them all morning.

He's older. He's old-fashioned. He's protective.

And yet — her father was also older, old-fashioned in many ways and cared about his daughters, but he had never suggested that any of them shouldn't take on a military career. Far from it, in fact. Tara had been happy with it, as had Izzie, but Azure...

Azure.

Azure had never wanted to join the military. Tara knew that now. She had bowed to family pressure, had been deployed, and had come back broken — and Liam was now the one to take care of her.

It didn't sit well in Tara's head. Liam the caretaker. Liam against what she had always loved. It was just all *wrong.*

And now to hear that he and Azure — That Azure had —

Fuck. Fuck, fuck, fuck.

There was a soft, gasping breath at the front of the room. Tara's eyes shot open involuntarily. Silently she turned her head toward the source of the noise, holding her body very still.

A familiar dark head was bowed at the altar.

Azure.

The gasping breath echoed again, and something stirred painfully in Tara's chest as she recognized the sound.

Azure was crying.

For a moment her heart warred with her head. After all that time apart, even now that they were talking again, she had no right to intrude on such a personal moment. And yet a deeper, more primal part of her refused to ignore that here was her sister, her twin sister, crying alone.

In the end, she went with her gut. The floor was lightly carpeted, silencing her steps until she was almost behind her sister.

"Azure."

Azure jumped, covering her face with her hand as she looked up. Her eyes were red, wide, lashes wet with tears.

"Tara! Give me a minute."

"I'm sorry, I just couldn't—"

Azure shook her head, digging a pack of tissues out of her pocket with her other hand. "I know. Just give me a minute."

Tara stood and looked away awkwardly as rustling, sniffling and nose-blowing went on beside her. After a few moments had passed, Azure got to her feet, flushed but thankfully dry.

"I'm okay now." Her voice was hoarse.

Tara felt that inner twist again at the sound. "I didn't mean to intrude. I was looking for somewhere private—I didn't know you were here. And then—" She broke off as Azure held up her hand.

"I can show you 'private'. Follow me."

'Private' turned out to be a boardroom right at the back of the yacht, its rear wall bisected by a long window looking out to the sea. Azure pulled out a chair and sat down, turning it to face the view.

"I didn't know this was here," Tara commented, leaning back in her seat.

"It's not somewhere you'd need to see. I've only seen it a few times myself."

"You've been on here a lot, then?" Somehow it was a question Tara had never thought to ask. She had simply assumed that Azure and the Sugiyamas had to be great friends—otherwise why would they have agreed to invite Tara, whom they had never even met?

"A few times. It's a business thing mostly. Tracey is a major arse-kisser, so we get invites every now and then."

Tara bit back a laugh at the image that sprang up. Azure threw her a grin.

"Oh, you have no idea how many star-fuckers I have to deal with."

Star-fucker. Tara kept a fake smile on her face as the word hit her like a slap.

"Where is Liam, anyway?"

Azure waved the question away. "Back in the cabin sleeping. He had a rough night."

"So did Kiki." Tara had been woken several times by Kiki pacing around the room, texting on her mobile phone. By the time she had left for breakfast, Kiki had finally been sound asleep, phone still in hand and an expression of strain on her face.

"Hmm." Azure raised a knowing eyebrow. "I'm not surprised. She had an...*energetic* evening."

Tara remembered Kiki dancing with Nik and the look of frustrated anger on his wife's face. "I don't think Tracey was thrilled about that."

"She never is." Azure eyed Tara with a teasing smile. "You and Ryan, on the other hand, looked like you were having a *great* time."

"Oh, shut up. You danced with him too."

"Only upright." Azure punched Tara lightly in the arm. "And he was very happy to get back to you. You didn't exactly look comfortable talking to Liam."

Tara blushed as memories of their conversation flashed through her mind. No, she had not been comfortable. Far from it.

"What were you two talking about, anyway? You looked very serious."

Oh God.

"Oh, you know. Tracey and her pregnancy," Tara lied, wondering if she had sounded as unconvincing as she felt.

Apparently she had. Azure's eyes darkened and she bit her lip.

"Ah, I see. He told you about me, then."

Every muscle in Tara's body felt as though it didn't belong. Her hand twitched as she battled with herself, torn between reaching out to Azure and keeping her distance.

"He thought I already knew."

Azure looked away, fixing her gaze on her fingers, which were twisting together painfully. "Figures."

"I'm really sorry."

Without raising her head, Azure gave an awkward shrug. "It happens."

"Do you know why? I mean—" Tara shook her head, struggling to find the right words. "*Is* there a why?"

"Don't know." Azure's voice had dropped, darker and strained. "After the first one, they just said don't worry. After the second one, they checked my meds, said keep trying. Gave me a full physical after the third." A long, weary sigh. "They didn't find anything."

Giving in to the urge, Tara tentatively reached out and rested her hand on Azure's shoulder. They sat silently for a few minutes, the only sound the distant slap of the waves outside the window.

A hundred useless, familiar platitudes were racing around Tara's head.

There's always the next time.

Just keep trying.

The doctors know best. If they say there's nothing wrong…

Ugh. As if any of that was going to help after three miscarriages. And somewhere, in amongst it all, was one throwaway line.

They checked my meds.

The image of Azure and her pills after their morning swim flashed into her mind. So many possible meds it could have been. Were they preventing her from carrying a child? Would it be safe to stop taking them—or would it make things worse?

Jesus. What a nightmare.

Azure brought her hands up to her face, rubbing her eyes, and Tara found herself speaking without thinking.

"He's very protective of you, isn't he?"

Azure cast her a sideways glance from under her hair. "Oh, you noticed?"

Bit hard not to. Tara bit off her response, but from the sardonic look in Azure's eyes, it had shown in her face.

"I guess I'm lucky. Not every man can deal with PTSD, you know."

"Yeah," Tara admitted.

"I'm better than I was. I was having panic attacks, had days when I couldn't go out. Liam got hold of the best doctors he could find, got me some therapy and meds. I still have nightmares, and some things still trigger flashbacks— Well, you saw..."

The press. Tara nodded, remembering the vacant look in Azure's eyes as the paparazzi had swarmed her.

"But I think he's just like that anyway. He likes to look after me."

"I guess so. But don't you find it a bit much sometimes?"

Azure's answer was cut off by the cheerful ring of her mobile phone. She retrieved it from her pocket, looked at the screen and smiled.

"Liam must have woken up." She hit the button and held the phone to her ear. "Hi, honey. Yeah, I'm down in the boardroom with Tara. I'll be right up."

Tara eyed her, forcing her face to remain blank. *Seriously? He couldn't have just waited for her?*

"Oh, I'm fine. No, I am, really. I'll be there in a few minutes. Okay, see ya." Azure dropped the phone back into her pocket and turned to Tara with a radiant smile.

"I guess you need to go," Tara offered helpfully.

"Yeah." Azure stood, pushing her chair under the table. "He wants to swim again before we dock tomorrow."

"Okay." Tara stood and followed her out of the room, a strange sick feeling lying in her stomach.

He was so damn protective. So— *smothering.* It was impossible for Azure to do anything without him checking that she was all right. Yes, Azure *was* delicate, and yet...

And the talk of miscarriages had left a painful twist in her gut, a memory, which made her just want to throw herself to the floor and scream and scream...

Taking a deep breath, she forced her own image of Liam Wilder back to the forefront of her mind—spellbinding, breathtaking Liam, exciting and unpredictable and ready to fuck her till she screamed.

That was it. *That* was him.

Any other sides of him vanished into the ether.

* * * *

It was beginning to feel as though all Tara's plans for the day were being overturned. First she had gone looking for solitude and had wound up deep in conversation with her sister, and now her plan to take her mind off Azure and Liam by spending the day with Ryan was being screwed up.

Things had begun well enough.

"Fancy grabbing an ice cream on the sundeck?"

Ryan had grabbed his sunglasses and sunblock before she had finished the sentence. "Hell yes."

It had been a beautiful afternoon. Ryan had waved away Tara's suggestion that he should bring a sunhat, but he had taken great pleasure in applying sunscreen to her back with some salacious massaging motions that had skated dangerously close to her breasts. Tara had returned the favor, making the obligatory comments about how muscular he was.

"No need to sound so surprised."

"Well, you're an accountant. You don't do biceps curls with a calculator."

"No, I do them with weights, thank you. Helps me fight off the assholes who bring me their taxes two days before the deadline."

After bringing two ice cream sundaes over, Ryan had returned to the subject. Apparently the 'accountant' dig had struck a nerve.

"Benefit of living in California is weather like this most of the time. When I get sick of finance I can go out and surf or play tennis."

Tara had eyed him over the rim of her sundae. Though she hadn't told him what kind to get, he had come back with a mojito sorbet drizzled in lime and mint syrup, which was enough to make her agree with anything he said.

"You do a lot of sports?"

"Yeah, when I can. We have an office basketball team and I go skiing with Nik a lot too." Ryan had picked up his own sundae, which had been so ablaze with orange segments and syrup that it had been almost blinding. "Do you?"

"I used to. Tennis, swimming, volleyball, that kind of thing. I don't really have time now for much except workouts."

Ryan had rolled his eyes. "You work too hard."

"Excuse me? I don't."

"You don't do *anything* that doesn't somehow feed into your career. I'm surprised you even have time to fuck."

Tara had given him a sardonic look. It had been on the tip of her tongue to point out that it was entirely the opposite—as far as men were concerned, she *only* had time to fuck.

No. That was a line of questioning she didn't feel like taking.

"I have plenty of time to fuck," she commented instead, arching her eyebrows. "I'll demonstrate later."

But two hours later, Tara had rolled over on her sun-lounger to see that Ryan was looking decidedly pale.

"Are you all right?"

Ryan had pressed a hand to his face—Tara had seen that his skin was glistening with sweat. "I think I've got a touch of heatstroke."

Tara had sat up. "We'll go back inside then."

"Yeah." Ryan had forced himself upright. "Think I might skip dinner tonight."

"Do you want me to bring you back anything?"

"No, I think I'll just try to sleep it off. You go do what you want tonight." Ryan had patted her thigh with his other hand. "I'll be better tomorrow."

So now Tara was sitting at dinner with Kiki, wondering what on earth was going through her roommate's mind. Kiki was again dressed to kill—her hair was elegantly styled in ringlets that fell over the straps of her gold halter-necked gown, but her makeup looked smudged and rushed. She was also eating her meal at a speed that suggested that someone was about to steal her plate.

"In a hurry?"

"Meeting someone," Kiki muttered through a mouthful of pasta.

Oh, great. Another person disappearing on her. Tara considered her options. Maybe an early night would be the way to go. At least she was likely to have the room to herself.

And yet somehow she felt restless.

It was, she decided, Kiki's fault. In spite of her silence, it was obvious that Kiki was on edge about something. She breathed rapidly, every few seconds brushing her hand through her hair. On more than one occasion had Tara looked up to see Kiki staring off into space, fork in mid-air and with eyes that looked suspiciously wet.

Maybe things weren't going well with the mystery man.

Tara slipped upstairs immediately after dinner and, finding the room empty as expected, picked up a book. But her thoughts were in a whirl, preventing her from taking in the words.

Ryan.

Liam.

Azure.

Ugh. She threw the book aside, lay back on the bed and slid her skirt up to her hips. If she was to be alone, she may as well enjoy it.

She was already wet—her fingers slipped inside her channel easily. Closing her eyes, Tara toyed with her moist folds and summoned up her favorite image. Liam on the edge of the deck, wearing only his swimming shorts, his chest bare—Liam smiling at her, approaching her—laying her down on her bed.

Oh, Liam.

Her clit pulsed under her thumb as she caressed herself, letting the fantasy develop. With her other hand she cupped her breast through her dress, feeling the nipple peak under her touch. In her head, as she slid her fingers in and out they were replaced with Liam's hard cock, thrusting into her over and over as she cried out for more.

Oh—

She screwed her eyes tightly shut as her movements increased, biting down on her lip to stifle her moans— she clenched down on her fingers as she felt every thrust of his cock gliding into her, again and again and *again—*

Ryan!

She came with a gasp, her eyes shooting open in shock as the image of Liam was abruptly replaced by blond hair, tanned shoulders and glinting, knowing green eyes.

What the hell had happened there?

Letting her hand fall away, Tara stared up at the ceiling, stunned, as the last vestiges of pleasure slowly faded away.

She had come thinking of Ryan. That was just — impossible to grasp. It had been Liam until the last few seconds then, as she had started to lose control, his image had vanished, forced out of the way by one so startlingly erotic that she had climaxed before she had had time to think.

Standing up, she felt the cabin spin. Suddenly the room seemed too confining. She had to get out. Pulling a wrap around her shoulders, Tara unlocked the door and stepped out onto the deck.

It was a clear night, starry and cool — in the darkness she could see constellations reflecting in the calm waves. She stepped over to the rail and rested her hands on the cold metal, letting the breeze rustle strands of her hair.

The stillness was peaceful. Tilting her head back, she lifted her eyes to the full moon, fantasizing for a moment that it was a spotlight. On stage yet with no one to see her. A slightly hysterical giggle escaped her. She was definitely not in her right frame of mind tonight.

As the image evaporated, she paused for a moment, listening — voices were approaching from her right, and the thought of being with people right then was unbearable. Her head was in a whirl. She needed to be somewhere quiet, somewhere nobody would bother her.

At least she knew she wouldn't run into Ryan. On instinct she slipped left and up the stairs to the top deck. Maybe the bar would be empty.

It was. In fact, she could see from outside that the upstairs bar was completely deserted. Tara tried the swing door and discovered that it was open. The room was surrounded by windows, and as she stood on the threshold the moon met her, casting an eerie glow over the room.

Darting inside, she made for the bathrooms at the far end of the room, meaning to splash her face and hands with water. A sudden wave of exhaustion washed over her, making her blink with fatigue.

She ignored the faint sound of voices coming closer.

Chapter Fifteen

Tara closed her eyes, resting her forehead on the cool surface of the mirror, and tried to stop her mind from spinning.

Too tired. Definitely. Time for her to go back to bed — her *own* bed, her mind automatically added. Not Ryan's — absolutely not.

You should check if he's feeling better, a voice in her head suggested.

Hell no.

She wasn't his girlfriend. She was his fuck, nothing more.

Without bothering to dry her hands, she made her way to the exit. As the first door closed behind her, she paused and listened intently. *What was that noise?*

Voices.

Kiki's and a man's.

Is this Kiki's mystery man? Pressing herself against the wall, Tara sidled up to the door to the bar, which was stuck open a crack. In the darkened space, the lit bar area was clearly visible, and she could just make out Kiki sitting at a table in the middle of the room.

The man was just out of view, but his voice was articulate.

"We can't meet like this anymore."

Oh no. Tara felt a pang of sympathy for Kiki. Forcing herself to be as silent as possible, Tara slid down the wall until her bottom touched the carpet then stretched her feet out in front of her. The last thing she wanted was for Kiki to realize that she was being overheard at what had to be a painful moment.

Not to mention a private one. But now was not a good time for her to walk out.

Kiki looked up at the unseen man, her face twisted in what looked more like anger than hurt.

"Sure we can. You want me, I want you. Why stop?"

"You know why," the man said firmly.

"I don't see why it changes anything."

"I have to think of my family."

What?

Tara bit back a gasp. This man had a family? Did that mean he was married?

Of course, he could be divorced, or have children from a previous relationship. It didn't necessarily mean anything. And yet—

A memory of the clay pigeon shooting range flitted through her mind, and Kiki's words came back to her.

'He's the one breaking his vows, not me. If he loved his wife he wouldn't do it, and if he doesn't, she should find someone who does. The mistress is the catalyst, that's all.'

"It's never bothered you before." Kiki's voice had lowered persuasively.

"For God's sake, Kiki! She's pregnant!"

Kiki stood, scraping her chair along the floor, the sound covering Tara's involuntary squeak of shock. In that moment, she had recognized his voice.

It was Nik Sugiyama.

Kiki was sleeping with Tracey's husband. Tracey who had just announced her pregnancy.

And Kiki didn't care.

"So what? You cheat on your wife for months and *now* you get an attack of morality?"

"Kiki—"

"No, Nik. Listen." Kiki moved to stand in front of him, reaching up to cup his face. "Remember what you said to me when we first got together?"

"Of course. It wasn't that long ago." Nik's voice was breathless.

"It was a year ago." One of Kiki's hands moved— Tara couldn't see where it went, but a gasp from Nik suggested at least one spot. "You told me that you loved her, but she didn't like sex. That she wouldn't blow you, or dress up for you, or let you fuck her in the ass. And that was why you liked *me*."

"I—"

"You know you still want me." Kiki's voice was low, sensual. "She doesn't need to know—"

"Kiki—enough. Stop." Nik stepped backwards, pushing Kiki's hands away.

"This doesn't affect your marriage—you told *me* that. Nothing has to change."

"Yes, Kiki. It does."

Heavy footsteps left the room. As the far door swung open, Kiki, who had been standing frozen, seemed to shake off her shock, knocking the table over to run after him. Her voice trailed behind her, "Nik, wait! Stop!"

Well, fuck.

Tara slowly leaned her head back against the wall, listening as the sounds of footsteps and the swinging door tailed off into silence.

She could barely believe it. That Kiki would…

And yet she should have, because hadn't Kiki said it herself? But even then, the pregnancy changed everything, surely?

Apparently, in Kiki's mind, it didn't.

Tara stood, carefully pushed the door open and peeped out, scanning the bar. Seeing that it was empty, she made her way to the exit. The stairs to the deck were deserted. Wanting to be alone, she headed downstairs, stepping out into cool night air.

The silence seemed to wash over her, broken only by the light slap of waves against the boat. She leaned over the railing, watching the moonlight glitter on the water.

So that was why Kiki had been acting so strangely all this time.

And her rivalry with Tracey, too. Had that always been there, or had it stemmed from this? Tracey certainly knew that Kiki flirted with her husband — suddenly the barbed comments and spiteful glances made sense. But did Tracey know what was going on? Or at least suspect?

God. If Tracey had known before the cruise, then it must have been Nik who had extended the invitation — and how much of a nerve did it take to invite your mistress on a cruise with your wife?

In a way she could understand Kiki's incredulity. In the circumstances Nik could hardly claim to be a paragon of morality. He had hidden it so well. But in her way Kiki had been right. No decent husband would do what Nik had done.

A piercing scream cut through the air.

What the hell? Tara gasped, clutching the railing — that sound had been *close*, and although her mind was still rattling through questions about *who* and *where*, the chill that ran through her body told her exactly where that physical pull was leading her.

Azure.

It had come from the porthole just a few feet away. Tara found herself in front of it within seconds — the room was dark, and for a moment she squinted, unable to see.

Then two figures on the bed began to emerge from the inky black, accompanied by heavy, sobbing breaths. One figure was kneeling, the other sitting up in bed. Liam had his arms around Azure, whose head was buried in his shoulder, and he was rocking her, murmuring something into her hair.

The sobbing gradually formed into words. Tara could vaguely pick out the words "I'm sorry."

"Don't be silly," Liam said firmly.

"I just — I just wish it would *stop* —"

"I know. I know."

"I keep *seeing* it —"

The figures shifted, as if Liam's arms were tightening. "Shhh. Don't think about it."

"I'm so sorry —"

"Honey, don't." Liam moved back, and Tara saw the outline of his profile as he rested his forehead against Azure's. "This is what I'm here for, and you know I'll *always* be here."

Moving as silently as possible, Tara took one step backwards, then another. When the rail pressed against her back she turned and moved, hand over hand, along it until she was at the very farthest end of the deck, unseeing, moving only by feel.

The image of Azure crying in Liam's arms refused to leave her. She hung her head over the railing, feeling the wind catch her hair and wondering how much weight it would take to pull her right over.

She's my sister. She needs him. And I'm trying to steal him.

Alone in the dark, she slid down onto the deck and huddled against the shield of the side wall.

I'm no better than Kiki.

Her room was no longer a safe haven. Kiki might have gone back there, and she couldn't face her — not like this. And Ryan...

Oh God, no.

All this time she had been using Ryan,

No. She could never use Ryan like that again.

The wind ruffled her hair, and Tara ducked, burying her face in her knees.

She didn't deserve him. She didn't deserve someone who had been nothing but good to her while she had been stringing him along, waiting for her chance to betray her own sister.

It was impossible. She could never see Ryan again.

* * * *

Chaos, terror, bursts of light and frantic screams.

It was the same scene she knew, over and over, and yet suddenly she found herself apart from it, concealed in a small space behind a wooden wall.

She had been here before. Lying back, staring through cracks in the wood, feeling something internal go — pain — shock — a rush of blood. She held herself very still, struggling to stay calm, to prevent some nameless horror from happening again.

The view was truncated. Feet running past, kicking up dust — the roar of an explosion, the pop of gunfire.

She should be outside. She should be helping. And yet somehow it was of vital importance that she stay here, stay safe.

Then something shifted inside her gut, and she remembered.

Chapter Sixteen

Above anything else, Tara wanted to be alone.

She had retreated to her room at three a.m. to find it empty. Obviously Kiki had still been at large, probably trying to convince Nik that he should stay with her. Curling up under the covers, she had pulled the duvet over her head and fallen into a fitful sleep.

At nine a.m. she had surfaced to find that Kiki had returned, her blonde hair on the pillow the only part of her visible. The thought of facing her, knowing what she now knew, was intolerable. Tara had dressed quickly and fled, closing the door as quietly as she could to avoid waking her.

Breakfast was out of the question. So was the gym. Azure might be in the chapel. In fact, it was the thought of Azure that led Tara to the one place she thought would be empty at this time of day.

The boardroom.

The lights automatically came on as she entered, but after a few minutes of no movement, they switched off again, leaving the room dull and apparently uninhabited. Tara sat in the corner nearest the door —

almost invisible to any passers-by — and rested her head against the wall.

God, it was a nightmare.

What the hell was she going to say to Ryan? How could she explain why she couldn't see him anymore? There was no way she could tell him the truth, no way at all.

You're a stone cold bitch. Reese had been right. *Oh God.*

Her thoughts were cut off by the sound of footsteps approaching. Tara pressed herself back against the wall as hard as she could, holding her breath. There was no reason for anyone to look in here, she reasoned. Surely even Nik wouldn't be needing it right now.

The footsteps stopped, the door opened, and Ryan's head appeared around it. "Ah, there you are."

Oh, for fuck's sake.

"How the hell did you find me in here?"

Ryan let the door swing shut as he strode toward her, positioning himself cross-legged on the floor in front of her. "It was Azure's idea."

Tara rolled her eyes. Ryan folded his arms and cocked his head to one side, looking at her with a cheerfully patient expression.

"Are you feeling better now?" Tara finally asked.

"Yes, thank you. And well done for avoiding the obvious."

"And what's the obvious?"

Ryan gave her a mock-exasperated look. "Why you're holed up in here."

For a moment, Tara felt the familiar burst of irritation — Ryan getting under her skin *again* — and her glare was met with that answering glint in Ryan's eye that she had come to know. But before she could fire back a reply, the realization closed in on her.

Because I'm a bitch who used you for sex while I was trying to steal my sister's husband.

She couldn't say that to him. But what could she say?

"Hey." Ryan's hand appeared under her chin, tilting it up.

Tara noticed for the first time that she had been hanging her head. As her eyes met his, a shock ran through her—he looked *worried.* Compassionate, even.

"Look. Something's obviously wrong. You don't have to tell me, but, you know, it might help."

I doubt that, Tara's mind automatically responded as she held his gaze. She didn't go in for asking for help, and certainly not from a man.

But something inside her was rebelling against that shield.

Maybe he deserved the truth. A part of it, at least.

She owed him that much.

It was an edited version, but it was still true.

With skin burning and fingers clenched around her knees, Tara finally let him hear the story of her estrangement from Azure. How she had let a childhood fascination and one brief one-night stand— one that even now Azure knew nothing of—create an attachment that, as she told him, sounded ridiculous. How she had allowed her jealousy to form a barrier against her sister—how their relationship, which she now could see had already been eroding, had been abruptly destroyed.

She couldn't bring herself to admit her current feelings for Liam or Ryan's place in her twisted game. But she knew she had made any attempt at reconciliation with Azure difficult, and she admitted that too.

The last, darkest secret, the one that she forced from her mind though it lay heavy in her gut, she kept to herself. To discuss it was still unbearable.

By the time she had finished, her head was resting on her knees again. The thought of making eye contact with Ryan was intolerable.

God knows what he thinks of me now.

A pointy finger poked her in the forehead. Reflexively Tara recoiled, lifting her eyes before she realized what she was doing.

Ryan was still sitting there, still looking at her with what she thought was an understanding expression, although the slight curl to his mouth suggested that he was now more amused than concerned. He raised his eyebrows as their eyes met.

"Now *that* I wasn't expecting."

"I'm sure you weren't." Tara bit her lip, looking away.

"Don't make me poke you again."

Tara slid her eyes back toward him. He was smirking.

"Yes, all right. I know it was stupid. Go on, tell me I'm a dumb blonde or something."

"I wouldn't dream of it, Golden Girl. I've seen what you can do to a punchbag."

Grudgingly Tara laughed, watching Ryan's face as his smugly twisted mouth curved into a friendlier grin. He was taking this much better than she had expected.

Of course, he didn't know the worst parts, but that was a humiliation she simply could not face. To have him know about her silly crush and petty reaction was bad enough.

"There is one thing I'm wondering, though," Ryan commented.

"What?"

"What set this off all of a sudden?"

Oh. Tara paused for a moment. "Kiki."

To her surprise, Ryan nodded. "You found out about her and Nik, then."

"You knew about that?"

"Oh yeah. Not from her, from Nik. Not much I could say about it to him, but he knew I thought he was being a dick."

"Yeah, well, I found out last night, and it made me feel like shit."

"I'd hardly put you in the same category."

You don't know what I was trying to do. Tara shrugged, avoiding his gaze.

"Hey." Ryan tapped her on the nose, making her grimace. "Having a thing for your sister's husband is one thing—fucking a married man is another. You're nothing like Kiki."

"If you say so."

"I do, and I'm always right, so stop arguing."

Tara threw him a patented dirty look, which had no effect on Ryan's grin whatsoever.

"Seriously. What can I say that will make you feel better?"

Something clicked in Tara's head. She looked at him steadily, feeling a new sensation building in her gut.

"You can't. But you can do something."

"What's that?"

Tara took a deep breath.

"Spank me."

* * * *

"Tell me you're sure about this."

"I'm sure."

Ryan's cabin door clicked shut behind them. His hand was already on the lock as he spoke, "No, I mean it. I don't want to be *punishing* you."

Tara looked him in the eye as the lock snapped closed.

"I know. I want this. Do it."

She pulled her shirt and bra over her head, before dropping them on the floor. Ryan was still watching her intently, making no move to undress himself. That was fine. It was fitting for her to make herself vulnerable while he stayed clothed.

There was a chair in the room, but she didn't think it would hold them both. It would have to be the bed. She stepped out of her trousers and knickers, leaving them in a heap, and looked back toward Ryan, who still stood in front of the door.

Watching.

For a long moment, neither moved. Then Ryan crossed to sit on the end of the bed, never taking his eyes off her. Tara stood in front of him, her breathing quickening in anticipation.

"How do you want to do this?"

Tara answered him immediately, "Across your knee."

When Ryan spoke, his voice caught in his throat. He coughed and tried again, "Come here then."

His jeans were rough against her thighs as Tara positioned herself across his lap. For a moment she was thankful that she was tall—her hands and toes rested on the floor, helping her to balance. She shivered, feeling completely exposed to him, her arse in the air, hair falling forward to conceal her face.

A warm hand caressed one cheek.

"Don't let me hurt you."

Tara let out her breath slowly. "I trust you." And in that moment, she realized that it was true. She did trust him — to discipline her without going too far, to give her what she needed.

"I'll give you twenty." His voice came again. "And if you say stop, I will."

Tara nodded, closing her eyes. The hand disappeared, and she stiffened, bracing herself.

"One."

Oh! Tara gasped as his hand came down hard on her right cheek, her body jolting with the shock. Sensation radiated out from the spot, her skin burning at the contact.

"Two."

The second blow landed on her left cheek. Inwardly Tara found herself approving of the degree of force. It wasn't pain so much as a sting, but he was going to make her feel it — good. That was what she wanted.

She was used to physical discipline, after all. Maybe not like this, but hell, it was better than doing drills for hours at a time. She knew she could take it.

And he deserved her submission.

She bit her lip as the third and fourth blows landed in quick succession, one on each thigh. With the fifth, he shifted position and switched hands. A memory of old-fashioned school stories flickered in her mind — *This is going to hurt me more than it will hurt you* — and she stifled a giggle, which turned into a moan of desire.

Because now it *was* desire.

The submissive position, the sensations rippling through her body — all were sending tingles along her nerves, making her gut tighten with excitement. Another smack made her gasp, digging her fingers into the floor, and as her thighs parted, the cool air on her cunt made her realize she was growing wet.

Maybe, after...

She shifted slightly on Ryan's lap and felt something hard poke her in her hip. A sharp intake of breath above her told her she had guessed correctly.

He likes this too.

Another smack, and Tara let herself go, crying out with every stroke and reveling in Ryan's answering moans. She could sense his muscles tensing, his cock hardening further as she wriggled on his lap, and she clutched at his ankle as her movements almost threw her off balance, her toes scraping the floor.

"Twenty." Ryan's hand landed softly on her bottom, stroking her tender skin.

For a long moment, Tara lay still, catching her breath. The gentle caresses to her abused cheeks felt like a reward for standing her punishment—although she would never use that word to Ryan. Standing her discipline, maybe.

Then one movement brushed a little lower, teasing the inside of her thigh, and Tara moaned, wanting his hand to slide farther down and to pleasure her properly.

"Ryan—" She twisted to face him.

Ryan stopped her with a hand to her shoulder. "Don't move."

"What—"

In answer, Ryan slid two fingers inside her channel. Tara groaned, letting her head fall back down.

"Just stay right there and let me handle it." He twisted his hand, moving his other fingers to press against her clit.

Tara stifled a cry against her fist. "Ryan!"

In response, Ryan pulled back then thrust his fingers in again, and Tara gave herself up to pleasure.

It was a strange feeling, and yet more exciting than she could have imagined. The throb of residual pain across her cheeks—with the delicious sensation created by his touch, the heat on her skin and the cool air on her pussy... Her gut was already tightening and she clung to his legs as she felt her climax building deep within her.

"Did you behave badly?"

Through the roar of her own breath in her ears she heard Ryan's voice, guttural with desire.

Oh God. "Yes."

"Have you been disciplined for it?"

Tara screwed her eyes shut as the bliss took hold of her. "Yes—"

"Then it's done, and you don't need to think about it again. You're forgiven."

"I—" Her cunt clenched around his fingers, and Tara's voice rose in a shriek. *"Thank you!"*

Then she collapsed limply across his knees, and felt him press a kiss to her shoulder.

You're forgiven.

She wasn't sure if she believed it, but she could feel it, and something inside her seemed to snap free.

If he forgives me, maybe I can forgive myself.

Chapter Seventeen

Sitting against the bathroom wall, one arm hooked around her bent knee, Azure rested her head against the tiles and forced herself not to look at the piece of white plastic on the floor beside her.

Results in two minutes, the box had said.

The conversation with Tara flickered in her head. It was odd to think that, after such a long period of coldness between them, she had been confiding in her sister about all the miscarriages, three of the most painful events in her life.

But she hadn't told her about this.

The doctors had advised against it. It was best not to tell anyone, family included, until she was past the three-month mark. Then she would be out of the most dangerous period, less likely to have another —

She checked her watch. One more minute.

Two years of trying without success. She would have done anything to make it happen. What had begun as instinct had become an ache. She *had* to have children. She *couldn't* stop hoping, even in the face of more and more setbacks.

She had done this so many damn times. So many times it had been negative. But at least that had been better than the gripping pain, the blood, and the knowledge of the life lost.

Definitely best to tell no one. Not even Liam. Though he had concealed it well, the loss had hurt him every time, and Azure couldn't stand to see the hope light up his eyes only to die again. It was worse than having to tell all the happy, congratulatory people that no, she was no longer pregnant, that once again—

She screwed her eyes shut, forcing the pain back.

She had left it a long time. If it was positive, she would have to be at least three months gone, possibly more. Not much longer to wait. Not much longer.

Oh, I hope…

Eyes still closed, she picked up the test and held it up. The instructions were burned into her mind. One line for not pregnant. Two lines for pregnant. So simple.

Please…

Be brave. Do it.

She opened her eyes, focusing on the object in her hand, on its little screen.

Two lines.

* * * *

"You really need to see this place. It's gorgeous."

Tara, her mouth full of bacon, simply nodded her head. She was sitting at breakfast with Azure. Her sister had been talking excitedly for the past half-hour about their trip ashore that morning, apparently unperturbed by the fact that Tara was eating while her own plate was empty.

She glanced across the room and spotted Liam making his way over with two breakfasts. Azure had decided to order off-menu—Tara had assumed that this would be no trouble for the wait staff, but Liam had insisted on going over to the kitchen to make sure that everything was perfect. It had taken all of Tara's self-control to avoid rolling her eyes.

Honestly, does he do everything for Azure?

It was a silly question. She had seen enough by now to know that he did. Azure never fetched her own drinks, food, towel or suntan lotion. She barely needed to lift a finger. And yet it didn't seem to be controlling at all. Azure made all her own decisions—Liam simply wrapped her in cotton wool the whole time.

"Did you say you'd been to Italy before?"

Tara swallowed her mouthful. "Yes, to Venice. Never to this end, though."

Azure leaned back in her seat as Liam reached over her shoulder to slip her plate on the table. "I love Calabria. Especially Praia a Mare. The coastline is just stunning."

As Liam settled down in his seat, Tara cast an eye over both their meals. Liam had a full English breakfast with poached eggs, very similar to her own. Azure, however, had ordered devilled eggs on toasted brioche with Parma ham and melted mozzarella.

"That just looks bizarre."

Azure shrugged. "It's my version of a Monte Cristo sandwich."

"If you say so. Sounds weird to me."

"Don't eat it then." Cutting off a piece of brioche, Azure flipped her hair back in a manner that suggested dismissal of both Tara and the conversation.

Tara threw another glance around the room. No sign of Ryan. She had left him in bed that morning—he often liked to sleep late. Over the past two weeks they had fallen into a rhythm. Frequently they would run into each other in the gym after breakfast—if not, she usually met him for lunch. Dinner depended on Kiki, but dancing was a given.

And the nights were a hectic blur.

Ryan was good with his hands, good with his tongue. He was athletic—often they would wrestle for position, taking it in turns to roll on top. He was strong enough to lift her so they could fuck against the wall, even strong enough to hold on after he came.

And when Tara wanted him to, he spanked her.

On more than one occasion Tara had spent breakfast fidgeting at the pressure of her seat against her sore arse. Today, thank goodness, her bottom was untouched. The thought of explaining it to Azure was unbearable.

Instead, she and Ryan had spent most of the night cuddling, something that had left Tara with a strange uncertain feeling.

She had never been a cuddler, and yet she had liked it.

Shaking the memory away, she looked up to see Liam getting up again.

"Is he off again?"

"Mmm." Azure paused, fork in the air. "Getting drinks."

Tara let out an exasperated breath. "You've got him well trained."

"I know." Azure's tone was airy.

This is ridiculous. I have to ask.

"Don't give me that. You let him do everything for you. Why?"

Azure was chewing, but as Tara held her gaze, the silence took on meaning.

"Why do you let him do that?"

The question hung in the air for a moment. Tara's eyes never left her face.

"You never needed to be taken care of. None of us did."

Okay, so this couldn't be avoided. Azure looked at Tara for a moment, considering her answer.

'Because of my PTSD' wasn't good enough. Tara knew about that already and clearly saw it as something to recover from. She couldn't see how it might change a person's life.

Because I need to be safe.

She had first recognized it the morning after she and Liam had slept together.

* * * *

Two years earlier

Waking up, she rolled over to see his tousled hair on the pillow. For a moment she let herself indulge, watching him as he slowly stirred to wakefulness. One eye opened and caught hers, then a slow smile spread across his face.

"Good morning. Are you hungry?"

As if it was listening, Azure's stomach immediately rumbled. Chuckling, Liam raised himself up on one elbow and pointed with the other hand to the bedside table.

"You can order breakfast on the laptop. It's connected to the kitchen."

Azure retrieved the laptop and rested it on her lap as she switched it on. Leaning over, Liam guided her through the menus until a list of breakfast items appeared on the screen.

"What would you like?" Azure asked.

Liam settled back down, his head propped on his hand, and smiled lazily up at her. "Why don't you decide?"

Ooh.

Azure turned back to the screen, ducking her head to hide the fact that she was grinning like a fool. Running down the list quickly, she hit the buttons for scrambled eggs, black pudding — which was labeled as 'blood sausage' — bacon and orange juice.

"Are you sure that's okay?"

Liam's smile was beatific. "There's nothing on there I don't like. It's my menu."

Of course. Idiot.

Azure scrolled to the bottom of the list and hit *send*. As the screen cleared, she noticed several other menu options in the sidebar. *Lunch. Dinner. Snacks. Drinks.*

"Can you order *all* your meals from up here?"

"Absolutely." Liam rolled onto his back and stretched luxuriantly, exposing a broad expanse of bare chest. "So if we don't want to, we don't ever have to leave the bed."

Azure echoed his movement, lying back against the pillows and letting her eyes drift closed. The duvet settled across her chest, warm without being suffocating, and as her muscles relaxed a curious sensation flushed through her limbs — a feeling of utter security.

Safe. I'm safe here.

Enveloped in softness, in warmth, supported at every angle. Someone to bring food whenever it was needed. And a man alongside her who was creating long-forgotten stirrings in her body, whom she already felt tied to inextricably.

In that one moment, there was nothing else she wanted.

She noticed it again a week later.

Plans for the wedding were already under way. Azure was lying on the sofa in the living room, notepaper scattered on the floor beside her. The dress designer had just left—the wedding planner was due in fifteen minutes. Lying back, Azure gazed dreamily up at the ceiling and let herself drift.

It was like being enveloped in a warm cocoon. Swirling patterns above, softness below. She rolled her head to the side and settled her gaze on the far window, which commanded a view of the private gardens. The glass, she already knew, was triple-glazed, muffling sound, a barrier from the world outside.

A flash of the previous night's nightmare sparked in her mind, and Azure shuddered.

Heat. Explosions. Noise. Blood.

You're safe. You're safe. You're safe.

No one could get into the garden—security was at its highest there. No one could get through the window. No one could get to her.

And I don't ever have to go anywhere if I don't want to.

If she chose, she could stay safe in this house for the rest of her life.

* * * *

As she explained, she could already see that Tara was having difficulty understanding.

"But...why would you *want* that? I thought you loved traveling."

"We do travel. That's not what I meant." Azure paused, trying to think of a better way to explain it. "I'm not a trailblazer like you anymore. I don't want to take any more risks."

Tara shook her head, either in confusion or denial. Azure sat back in her seat and watched her mull things over.

Probably Tara had had her own thoughts about life with Liam. Nothing based on reality, of course. To her, Liam had always been the intellectual jackrabbit and physical firecracker from his commercials. The idea of him being a real person was probably beyond her.

Or, possibly, the idea of him not being her type.

Her thoughts flitted to Ryan. Now there was a man who could manage Tara, who could match her mentally and physically without smothering her or boring her.

Did Tara know this?

No point telling her if she doesn't. She'd dump him just to be difficult.

"Don't you want to be taken care of sometimes?"

Tara blinked, as if she had lost her train of thought. "No. I don't need taking care of."

"I said want. Not need."

"Still no." Tara folded her arms and leaned back in her chair, angling herself away from Azure. "I don't like relying on other people. You know I don't."

"There's nothing wrong with letting someone else take the weight occasionally, you know. I'm sure Ryan would—"

A strange expression crossed Tara's face. She held up one hand sharply, cutting Azure off. "Yeah, I'm sure Ryan would love that. But I would *never* submit to him. Never."

Never what? "Submit to him? Who said anything about that?"

The look on Tara's face changed instantly from righteous anger to 'oh fuck'. *Oh*, this was going to be good.

"I didn't mean—I mean he doesn't get to take charge."

"Riiight." Azure tried and failed to contain a grin. Tara turned an interesting shade of pink.

"He doesn't."

"Oh, I don't know. I think he'd make a great dominant."

"Shut the fuck up."

"No, I think you'd look good in handcuffs."

Tara flushed almost scarlet. Her reply was cut off by the creak of the bar door—Liam was on his way in with the drinks.

Ah, well. Azure resigned herself to dropping the subject, but allowed herself the pleasure of leaning in to whisper in Tara's ear first.

"Sub."

"*Fuck off!*"

* * * *

It was a beautiful day.

Tara leaned over the rail as the rumble of the tender's engine cut through the air. She glanced over at Kiki, who was leaning back against one of the lifebelts, staring coldly off into space. Although as far as Tara knew, the situation was still mostly private— the other guests were keeping their distance, avoiding the forcefield of hostility that radiated from her.

She had been like that ever since that night.

Tara had barely spoken to her. In the mornings Kiki was still buried under the covers when Tara left — she would occasionally surface for dinner, but would wolf down her food and immediately leave, and would be already asleep when Tara returned to the cabin. She avoided company whenever possible, and when she did appear — like now — she maintained a stony silence, repelling every friendly overture with a glare and a one-word answer.

Why she had come out to go ashore was anyone's guess. Tara had thought it would be a good chance for her to be completely alone while everyone else was off the boat. Maybe she just wanted a change of scenery from her enforced solitude. Or maybe she was just keeping up appearances, although, in that case, she was doing a poor job.

Apparently noticing Tara's glance, Kiki looked up and glowered. Hastily Tara looked away. Probably best not to engage with her. She turned toward Ryan, who was inching closer and closer to the steps.

"In a hurry?"

Ryan threw her a grin. "I like to go first. In everything."

"Not in *everything*, I hope," Tara shot back, remembering their interlude that morning. That had definitely been an incidence when Ryan *hadn't* gone first.

Ryan raised an eyebrow. "Well, you'd know, Golden Girl."

Tara's reply was cut off by the thud of the rope hitting the lower rail as the pilot tied up the tender. A sudden crack rang out, followed by a curse. The boat pitching in the choppy water had caused the rope to snap.

"Shit! Hold on, everybody." The pilot began digging around in the bottom of the boat. Shaking his head, Ryan pushed himself away from the rail.

"While he's sorting that out, I forgot my sunglasses. Don't go without me."

"Sure."

As Ryan left, Tara crossed to the bow and leaned over the side, straining to see any glimpse of the town. Azure joined her at the rail.

"What're you looking for?"

"Trying to see Praia." Tara looked up at her. "In case there are crowds."

Azure shrugged.

"You think it'll be okay this time? With the press, I mean?"

"It was in Lloret, so fingers crossed. I'm so sick of being under high security."

Tara rolled her eyes in sympathy.

"We can't do a damn thing at the moment. Liam can't even meet the public anymore."

"Those meet and greets?" Tara asked, the words coming out without thinking.

"Yeah, he stopped doing them about two years ago. Pity, they were really popular." Azure glanced across at her. "I was a bit surprised you never went to one, to be honest. He used to do them all the time."

"I did."

"When?"

"I was about twenty-two. You were deployed." Tara shrugged, trying to look casual. "He doesn't remember me."

She had thought it a harmless thing to admit—after all, what harm was there in a simple meet and greet? But Azure was staring at her, her face paling, and the slow realization began to dawn on her.

That maybe she hadn't been unique. Maybe, before Azure, 'meet and greets' had had a different meaning.

And maybe she looked guiltier than she had intended.

"*Should* he?" Azure finally asked, and the tone in her voice sent a cold rush to Tara's gut.

Oh God.

"I—"

Azure turned away abruptly, one hand covering her face, and Tara winced.

"Azure, I—"

"Why didn't you *tell* me?" Though whispered, the question was almost a wail.

"I was ashamed."

"Why? You were never ashamed of one-nighters. And with *him*—?"

And there was no way out—no way to avoid it.

Just as there had been no way to avoid it when, two months after that disappointing day, Tara had locked herself in her parents' bathroom and forced herself to admit the inevitable.

* * * *

Four years ago

She was nauseated all the time. Her breasts were tender, uncomfortable. And she was late—her body usually ran like clockwork. She had been denying it for days, cursing herself for her lack of care. Why had she taken the risk? Why hadn't she insisted on a condom?

The piece of plastic in her hand had told her the truth she had been dreading.

One line for not pregnant. Two lines for pregnant.

Two lines.

She had told nobody, instead spending hours in her room agonizing over the decision. She was single. Twenty-two years old. She was dedicated to her career. She simply couldn't face the idea of having a baby. The thought of her mother's shock and her father's disapproval paled into insignificance behind the image of herself alone and penniless, left to bring up a child as a single parent, the empty years of her life stretching ahead of her.

But it was Liam Wilder's baby.

She couldn't tell him. Even if she could somehow get in touch with him — and by now she knew he had gone back to America — what would he do? Pay her off? Or maybe she would end up dragging him through the courts, painted as a gold-digging whore by the press. Oh God, she couldn't bear it.

But it was *Liam Wilder's* baby. Could she really abort his child?

In her head, she imagined contacting him, hearing him tell her how happy he was, that he would support her. Herself pregnant, feeling the baby move and kick, Liam beside her. It was a wonderful fantasy, but every time she indulged herself, it would dissipate in the face of reality — of loneliness, poverty, family disgrace.

It would never happen. What she dreamt of was an impossibility. But aborting his child — her body rebelled against the idea.

She couldn't decide what to do.

The two impossible choices had hovered over her head for days. Her mother kept asking her if she was ill — Tara hated herself for causing her worry. Her next deployment loomed on the horizon, and she knew that somehow, some way she would have to bite the bullet.

In the end, the decision was taken out of her hands.

She woke up in the middle of the night, pain in a tight band around her stomach. Bleeding. Tara made her own way to the military hospital, not daring to wake her parents. Once there, it was confirmed. A miscarriage.

Her troubles were over.

Except they weren't.

She had forced the memory back, told no one, kept on going. And somehow, as the pain eased, it became a precious connection with him. She was able to dream about him again, fantasize, with the remembrance of what had happened partitioned off in a neat little box.

He was outside of her world, and so was their baby.

Until Azure had married him.

* * * *

Her voice had cracked as she had finished speaking.

Through the ringing in her ears Tara could hear the pilot calling people back to the tender, and she would have thrown herself head first into it rather than know she was the cause of that terrible look on Azure's face.

"Azure—"

The words were broken, forced through her sister's teeth.

"Leave me alone."

And Azure turned and walked away.

With the rope secured, the guests moved forward and loading began.

Tara kept her gaze averted as Liam and Azure made their way toward the steps. Ryan was behind her, sunglasses now in hand. Obviously not *that* desperate to be first, then.

The sea was calm, the tender rocking lightly with the waves. Tara positioned herself in the seat farthest forward, so her back would be to all the other passengers. Ahead she could see a glimpse of white beach peeking out from behind a cliff face, dazzling in the sun.

A memory of another coastal town, another rock face, flickered in her mind. Automatically she turned in her seat. Azure and Liam had sat down directly behind her, Liam with his arm draped around Azure's shoulders. Tara turned back as Ryan sat down beside her, struggling to quell the concerns shouting in her head.

Oh God, Azure, I –

Then another thought found its way through.

Paparazzi again? Has it been kept quiet this time?

Her stomach twisted as the engine roared and the boat began to scythe through the water. Surely nobody would know this time. Surely nobody could have found out. She was being ridiculous.

A minute later they rounded the curve into the bay, and Tara's heart sank.

The entire dock was crowded with people. A barrage of shouts rose as the boat came into view—"Mr Wilder! Mr Wilder!" Cameras were flashing, and behind her Tara heard Azure catch her breath.

"Turn around!" Liam ordered. The pilot nodded, and Tara slid in her seat as the boat began to turn in a curve, bringing itself side-on to the dock.

A sudden cry rang out, then another—outrage? Fear?—before somebody screamed, and a figure burst through the crowd. Tara's eye was immediately drawn to the familiar—too-familiar—shape in their hand.

A gun.

At this angle, Azure was directly to her left. Reacting without thinking, she threw herself sideways, ready to block—

A crack rang out, and Tara was knocked backwards into the space between the benches. Above her, voices cried out.

What the hell—

Then the pain in her shoulder hit her, and it all became clear.

I've been shot.

Chapter Eighteen

The world was spinning, voices clamoring over her head.

"Ryan. Hold this and press down there."

It was Azure's voice. A hand pressed down on her shoulder and Tara moaned as pain shot through her.

"I know, honey," the voice crooned. "You're going to be okay."

"The bullet's still in there." *Ryan.* "Shouldn't we—"

"No. It could be plugging an artery for all we know. Just keep pressing down."

In the background a radio was crackling. Another voice—the pilot—was speaking. Tara caught the word "chopper" and felt a ludicrous desire to giggle even as her vision began to blur.

"Can you move your hands for me, Tara?"

Azure's voice cut through her haze again.

Can I what? Were her hands even attached? Sluggishly she attempted to move one, her fingers dragging across the floor of the boat, and gasped as another jolt of pain hit her shoulder.

"That's good. Looks like your spine is okay. Liam, she's cold, could you —"

"Sure." Something weighty landed across her, something that felt like a blanket.

"Can you feel any air moving, Ryan? If it's a sucking wound we'll need to —"

"*No.* No, there's nothing."

There was a definite tremor in Ryan's voice. Bracing herself for more pain, Tara shifted her hand in the direction of his voice. It landed on firm flesh — his thigh, maybe? — and she attempted a comforting squeeze.

Laughter, slightly breathless. "It's okay, Tara. Don't worry. It's okay."

He didn't call me Golden Girl.

Another sound made itself known, gradually getting louder. Through the haze Tara could see a dark shape overhead, hear the steady *whomp* of helicopter blades.

"Everyone move back," she heard Azure say. "Give him space."

The boat bobbed as figures moved around her. Above her a figure seemed to be floating, gradually lowering toward her. Somewhere in the back of her mind the explanation suggested itself — a crew member being winched down from the helicopter.

"There's too much blood." Ryan, again.

"Here, use this." The pressure vanished for a moment then reappeared. Tara guessed that another cloth was being added. The boat rocked again as Liam stood, making space for the crewman, who had reached them and looked to be unfastening the line from his harness.

"Stretcher's on its way down," Azure was saying. "Okay, be ready, Ryan. We need to keep her steady when we move her."

"I'm on it."

There was a thump as something heavy landed in the boat, swinging on its line. Figures moved again, standing, reaching out to steady it. The pressure on her shoulder seemed to change, as though someone else was taking over. Tara felt hands tucking under her knees and ribs before she was lifted, her head supported against a warm body behind her.

"It's okay, Tara," Azure whispered as the rough fabric of the stretcher brushed against her back. "We just need to strap you in and you'll be on your way."

For a moment Tara wondered what it would be like to be winched up on a stretcher. She had never had to do it before.

She was still wondering when darkness overtook her.

* * * *

A white, sterile hospital corridor. Gray, squeaky flooring. A hard-backed seat. Azure leaned against Liam's arm, staring at the door in front of her and slowly untangling her thoughts.

God, she hated hospitals. The last time she had been in one, whilst having the stitches in her forehead, she had been on the verge of a panic attack the whole time. The muted colors, the rattle of trolleys, the echoing clop of shoes— Within a few minutes she would find her chest tightening and a cold sweat breaking out all over her body.

She knew why. It reminded her too much of the military hospital.

Lying in a hard, narrow bed, attached to IVs and nose tubes, and terrifying machines that went bleep. Being poked and prodded by doctors and nurses, having injections and sutures and at one point the indignity of a catheter. Being asked dozens of embarrassing questions, the doctor's manner cool and impersonal, as if her body were something disconnected from herself.

Then the visit from her commanding officer, and that one word she had hoped for and dreaded at the same time.

Discharged.

She'd had no desire to remain there. But at the time she'd had no desire to do anything. The journey home had been a blur. She had arrived at the base in a fugue state, walked past her father in the doorway and lain down on the couch with no plans to ever get up again. She had expected more questions from him, but none had come—she had eventually decided that he had already been briefed, either that or put on notice by her mother. Often she had looked up to see her father standing in the doorway, watching her with a strange expression that, on anyone else, she would have taken for sympathy or pity.

On him it had probably been constipation.

Liam tightened his arm around her, squeezing, and Azure returned her thoughts to the situation at hand.

Someone had shot at them.

Them. They still didn't know if she or Liam had been the target. Of course, it could have been neither of them, but at this point it was most likely, and, without confirmation from the police, Azure found it easiest to just assume the worst.

And Tara had taken the bullet.

In the moment the shot had rung out, Azure had frozen. Every muscle of her body had been paralyzed, electrified with those memories of *noise* and *heat* and *blood* and it had all been too much—a second longer and she would have been lost.

Then she had become aware that Tara had fallen, that the figure forcing itself in front of her had been her sister and that she was then in the bottom of the boat, bleeding from the left shoulder.

The adrenaline had flowed through her in one cold surge, bringing with it the memories of her field first-aid training, and before she had known it the panic had gone, replaced by the sort of urgent calm she had thought she would never need again after leaving the military.

She had thought she would lose all control, and instead she had taken charge.

Because it was Tara.

In that moment, all other thoughts had fled. Now, with time to think, they came flooding back, along with a heavy sick sensation in her gut.

Tara had slept with Liam.

Okay, so it had been before Azure had met him. And it had been a throwaway one-nighter—Liam didn't even remember her. But still, Tara had slept with *her husband*.

And she had fallen pregnant by him. The thought clutched at her heart. She could have had his child, contacted him. Maybe they would have even—

But it hadn't happened, she reminded herself. Liam was hers. He had never been Tara's.

And Tara had miscarried. A reluctant sympathy flickered inside her. She knew that experience. Knew the pain.

And Tara had taken a bullet for her.

Azure closed her eyes for a moment as a wash of resentment flooded through her. She knew it was unreasonable, but a little voice was shouting in her head. *You fucked my husband and I can't even be mad at you, you bitch! It's not fair!*

As if reading her mind, Liam tightened his arm around her, and the rage settled.

It didn't matter. None of it mattered.

Liam was hers. And Tara was Ryan's. Azure glanced briefly to her right, where Ryan was sitting on an equally uncomfortable-looking seat, slumped against the wall. He had held his nerve well. All the way to the hospital, right up until they had reached her room, he had maintained an almost eerie coolness that she had respected — he clearly didn't want to talk, so she had left him alone. It wasn't until they had been told that the worst was over that he had relaxed, and even now he was still in a world of his own.

Tara had no idea what she had. He was obviously crazy about her.

But then, it was Tara. So bloody determined to stand alone, so insistent that she didn't need a man except for sex — the only man she had ever let herself be irrational about was Liam. She would never let herself see that here was a man she could know for *himself*, not a celebrity only known from a photograph. A man who could complement her — who wouldn't weaken her as she feared, who would love her back.

Who would be far better for her than Liam.

Liam. At least Tara seemed to be getting a more sensible view of him. Maybe she was finally seeing that he was just a man, not a TV image. Just a man who, apparently, did far too much for Azure, if Tara's comments had been anything to go by.

She'll never understand us.

Maybe she didn't have to.

The sound of footsteps approaching broke into her musing. She looked up to see Nik coming toward them, closely flanked by two police officers. At the look on his face, she felt her stomach drop.

"Nik?" Liam asked, standing to face him. "What is it?"

Nik stopped, started to say something, then shook his head, covering his face with his hands.

* * * *

The first thing Tara noticed as she opened her eyes was the dull ache in her shoulder.

The second was the figure beside her bed, watching her with intent eyes.

"Welcome back," Azure said.

"How long was I out?"

"Few hours. How much do you remember?"

Tara closed her eyes in thought, seeing and hearing the chaos again—the glaring sunlight, the clamoring voices thick with fear. "All of it, I think."

"Good." Azure paused then rolled her eyes. "Well, not good, but you know what I mean."

"Where's Ryan?"

"He's outside. I'll go and get him in a bit." Azure's mouth twisted in a wicked smile. "He's been going nuts, poor guy. You might want to hold his hand or something."

Tara laughed, then winced.

"Careful. That nurse will kill me if you break your stitches."

Tara bit back another laugh, turning it into a smile. "I haven't seen her yet. Is she that bad?"

"Terrifying. Though not as much as Liam. He's talking to the police now. He's been *rabid* about this, talking lawsuits and everything."

At the mention of Liam, Tara's body chilled.

"Was it him they were aiming at, or you?"

Azure shrugged. "We don't know yet."

Her tone was casual, but her fingers were twisting together in a way Tara recognized, and Tara felt a sudden need to reach out to her.

"Are you all right?"

"Me? I didn't get—"

"Azure," Tara cut off the overly brittle response, fixing her sister with a look.

Azure held her gaze for a moment then looked away. "I'm fine. We might have to cut the trip short, though. Liam's not happy about our security. I'll talk to him about it when he sends the police in here."

Tara grimaced before she could stop herself. *Great. Just what I need.* "How did the press find out where we were going? I thought you were being more careful now."

Azure cast her a sidelong glance, her mouth twisting sardonically.

"We were. I gather Captain Matt has to report where he docks, but he's been being rigid about what he gives out."

"So how did they know?"

The look on Azure's face was almost deadly. "Ah, yes."

"What?"

"Turns out we had an informant on board."

"*What?*" Tara stared at her, her mind spinning. "Someone on the boat planned that?"

Azure shook her head briefly. "No, I don't think they planned the shooting. I don't know all the details yet, but it looks like a business thing. A former associate or something—a nutjob with connections."

She had said it so calmly, and yet under it was a current of steel. Tara waited.

"No, I mean the paps. Someone called ahead and told them."

"Do we know who?"

Azure rolled her eyes, an insouciant gesture at odds with the tension in her body.

"Tracey."

Chapter Nineteen

"Tracey?"

In shock, Tara sat up in the bed and winced as pain shot through her shoulder. Azure shook her head indulgently.

"Lie down, you idiot."

Tara lay back grudgingly. "Why would Tracey do that? I thought you were friends. I mean, that's why you're here, right?"

"Wrong."

For a moment all Tara could do was stare at her. *Wrong?* She had assumed that Azure and Liam were close friends with their hosts—close enough to have secured an invitation for her, even though they had never even met. So how could this now be wrong?

"It's complicated." Azure paused for a moment then screwed up her face. "Actually, it's not. Nik and Liam do business together, but they're also friends. Tracey and I—not so much. She likes to kiss up to Liam, but she gave up doing that to me a *long* time ago."

"Okay, but why did they invite you here if she hates you that much? Why did they invite *me?*"

"Ah." Azure raised a finger. "That's where it gets complicated."

Oh God. Tara could feel a headache coming on.

"You're right, she does hate me. That's why she kept setting the press on us. She knows it fucks me up, the bitch." A brief flash of anger darkened Azure's eyes before she went on. "But she also owes me and Liam big time, and it kills her. That's why she invited us."

"Owes you? You mean money?"

"No—although that did fit into it. We know something she doesn't want told."

Tara waited for her to continue, but Azure simply sat and smiled at her, obviously enjoying her impatience.

"*What?*"

"She came to see Liam about a year ago. Wanted to borrow some money. She had some major credit card debt she didn't want Nik knowing about. Liam politely told her to forget it. She got a bit desperate. I was listening outside, so I went in to rescue him."

"And?" The look of exasperated smugness on Azure's face was driving Tara crazy.

"And I walked in—just in time to see her drop to her knees and go for his zipper."

"Oh my God."

A brief image flashed into Tara's head of herself walking into an office to see Ryan in that position, Tracey on her knees in front of him. Her gut clenched almost painfully. How could Azure be *smiling*? Even knowing that her husband was entirely innocent, surely—

But then, it had been a year ago. Maybe a year's worth of reassurance from Liam and power over Tracey had dulled the memory into one only of amusement.

"So she invited you to—what, make it up?"

"Pretty much. To suck up." Azure's voice took on a mocking quality. "Oh pretty please, don't tell Nik, I'll do anything. You can come out on our yacht, it'll be such fun. Oh, please."

"I'd have told her to go fuck herself."

"I nearly did. In the end I told her we would come on one condition. That she invited you."

"That she…" Tara paused as this sank in. "Why?"

"You know why."

Tara opened her mouth to respond then closed it again.

She did know why.

Azure was her twin, her closest sister. Their relationship had been broken almost beyond repair. And it had been *her* fault, not Azure's. Azure had been blameless, yet she had been the one to hold out the olive branch.

She had done what Tara should have done.

"Why didn't you just invite me to America? Or set up a trip yourself? Why all this?"

Even as Tara said it, she knew the answer.

"You would never have agreed to that." Azure looked away. "I thought this would be less intense. More people, more places to see. Not just me and Liam."

It was impossible for Tara to deny.

"Azure, I—" *Say it.*

"I'm sorry."

Azure held her gaze for a moment, a soft smile touching her mouth, then gave one decisive nod, reaching out to take Tara's hand at the same time.

Automatically Tara went to meet her grasp then stopped abruptly as her shoulder reminded her of its painful existence. Azure laughed, pushing Tara's hand back onto the bed.

"Keep still, you fool. You're a crap patient."

Tara grimaced. "If I ever get hold of that arse with the gun, I'll strangle him."

"Get in line. The police have him, anyway."

"Just like that?"

"Like I said, nutjob with connections. Doesn't look like he planned past the actual shot."

Tara watched her with a sense of wonder. Azure looked so calm, so relaxed about it all. As if she was used to having crazy people shoot at her every day.

And that couldn't be right, could it?

"Why are you so calm? You have PTSD. Wouldn't this trigger you?"

The look Azure turned on her was beatific.

"I thought that too. But the only thing I could think of was saving your life."

"And the guy?"

Azure shook her head, still smiling.

"He's not important. What's important is that you took a bullet for me. I really don't care about anything else."

Unable to find the words, Tara simply squeezed her sister's hand.

There was really nothing else to be said.

* * * *

"You look like a nurse's nightmare."

Tara flashed Ryan a wry look and an obscene gesture as he popped his blond head round the ward door before walking in. It had been a day since she had seen him. Azure had left her alone to have lunch, and now Tara was discovering how much she hated being stuck in a hospital bed.

"I hear you're a terrible patient. Your nurse is going to need to check herself in by the time you check out."

"Thank God it won't be for long. They say I'll be up and about in a week."

Ryan sat down on the chair next to the bed, eyeing her knowingly. "Just long enough for you to recover without murdering anyone."

"I don't *do* lying around. It's driving me mad."

Laughing, Ryan leaned across the bed and kissed her firmly. Tara tilted her head back, relaxing as his tongue flickered across hers.

It was good to have something else to think about.

Sitting there, in a strange bed in an empty room, she had too much time to consider how long a full recovery would take. How long it would be before she could return to work. She had seen gunshot wounds before, seen other soldiers go through months of physiotherapy to get back up to speed.

She didn't like feeling so vulnerable. She didn't like knowing that some lunatic had done this to her. She *really* didn't like being in pain every time she moved her bloody arm.

And the damn bullet was still in her shoulder. Apparently it was too dangerous to remove it. It struck her as singularly ironic that, after all her tours of duty, she had gotten shot while on vacation.

"Want to know something funny?"

Tara blinked, looking up at Ryan, who had pulled away and was standing over her. "What?"

"Kiki's bouncing off the walls. Nik gave Tracey her marching orders, and so she thinks she's in with a chance."

"Nik gave..." Tara blinked again, wrestling her brain back into gear. She had understood, from a conversation with a police officer earlier that morning, that nothing legal was likely to be done to Tracey, since it appeared that she had had no involvement with the gunman. But then, while it was perfectly legal to tip off the press about where Liam Wilder was going to be, Nik was unlikely to have taken kindly to the idea.

Neither would Liam, of course, and if Nik valued Liam as a business connection... But then was that in itself a good enough reason to divorce your pregnant wife? Maybe, given that Nik was the kind of man to invite his mistress on a cruise with his wife and friends. Not exactly the poster boy for functional marriage.

Well. That was going to be an interesting divorce case, with Nik's billions and Tracey pregnant. Frankly, she thought Kiki would be better off out of it.

"*Is* she in with a chance?"

"God knows." Ryan grimaced. "Personally I think it's kind of tacky, but I'm past expecting class from any of those three."

"Good point. Let them get on with it."

Sitting down, Ryan took her hand and covered it with his. Tara threw him a smile as the contact sent a warm thrill along her spine.

She had never seen herself as the hand-holding type, and yet when it was Ryan...

Well, that was it, wasn't it?

Liam's comfort—and she knew it *was* comfort—would have been stifling, because for him hand-holding came with so much more—coddling, overprotection, waiting on a woman hand and foot. Ryan's comfort was nothing more than that. It was comfort in the moment, because that was what she needed—and she knew he would do anything else if she asked—but he would push her, and challenge her, and let her do whatever the hell she liked.

And spank me if I need it.

The thought sent a flush to her cheeks, and she realized she was watching Ryan with a look of unbridled lust—a fact that he was now aware of, as he was looking back at her with a raised eyebrow.

"Now that's a look I didn't expect from someone in a hospital bed."

Tara arched her eyebrow at him. "Just because my shoulder's fucked doesn't mean nothing else is working."

Ryan flashed her a heated gaze. "Don't worry. As soon as the week's up I'll take care of your needs."

"Oh, 'needs', is it? I'd call it 'wants', actually."

"Ohh, I forgot. Golden Girl doesn't have needs."

"Exactly." Tara cocked her head at him playfully. "Never needed anyone in my life."

Ryan shook his head, laughing. "You liar. You need me. Look what happens when you're left to your own devices. You go leaping in front of bullets and saving people's lives."

"Oh, that's nothing. You'd better get used to it."

Ryan eyed her indulgently. "You're crazy. Do I need to put you over my knee?"

Tara waggled her eyebrows at him suggestively.

"You'll have to work hard to get me there."

"I like a challenge." Ryan held her gaze for a moment. "You do know that I love you, right?"

It was unexpected, and Tara hesitated.

How do I answer that?

It was a situation she had never been in before. Not doing boyfriends by extension meant not doing love—

and God, that sounded depressing, to know that she had never been loved by a man.

She had never needed to answer a question like that. Did she know how she felt well enough yet?

In that moment, she knew that she did.

"I—"

"It's okay," Ryan cut in. "You don't have to say it back yet."

This time her response came immediately, "That's all right. I'll just think it then."

* * * *

The scene was the same, yet different.

As Azure she ran, as dust clouds formed and debris fell, she was aware of footsteps alongside, a figure in the space beside her. Behind them their pursuers were shouting, but the sounds were muted. All importance seemed to be tied to the shape nearby, running in step with her.

The terror seemed to be fading, left behind them as they ran.

A sudden crack from behind her, and her voice rose in a scream, but there was no pain, no force — only a firm grip on her shoulder, pulling, and she fell to one side, hitting the ground with a thud.

Sand was gritty under her skin, in her eyes, but in a blink her vision cleared.

Dark hair — her own — fell in front of her face. As she looked to the side, searching for her rescuer, she caught a glimpse of more hair — this time blonde.

Blonde hair, blue eyes, and a bright, white-toothed grin.

Saved.

Chapter Twenty

It was late in the afternoon when Tara returned to the yacht.

As she struggled one-handed up the steps to the deck, Ryan's hands resting protectively on her waist, she found herself wondering what she would face when she got there. Would there be a fuss? People rallying round her? Would the other guests fall silent and stare as she walked past?

Would Kiki still be her roommate, or would she have moved in with Nik by now? Had Tracey already left? God, Tara hoped so. She *really* didn't want to face the woman who was indirectly responsible for her injury.

She didn't particularly want to face Nik, either. The one visit he had made to her hospital bedside had been bad enough. 'Guilty' didn't even begin to describe it. He had almost burst into tears at one point. Tara had never enjoyed seeing men cry, and she would be happy never to see it again as long as she lived.

As she reached the deck, she glanced around for signs of life. In the distance she spotted a familiar blonde head and inwardly cringed. Regan. Of course she would be here. This sort of thing was her bread and butter.

Oh well. May as well let her have her fun.

"Oh fuck," Ryan murmured behind her, and Tara concealed a grin behind her hand. At least she would have some support in dealing with the barrage of questions.

Regan was approaching fast, and Tara braced herself. However, as she did so, another familiar figure slid into view at the far end of the yacht. Before she could think, he spotted her, turned his back and left.

Her gut tightened. This was something she would have to make right.

Reese.

* * * *

It was difficult to know what to say to him.

A small part of her still felt that she had done very little wrong. She had never promised him anything more than a one-night stand, or a one-morning stand in their case. And she hadn't expected him to want any more than that.

But, for whatever reason, he had. And she had hurt him.

There had been too much pain caused by mistakes and misunderstandings on this boat. She needed to resolve this with him.

She had seen very little of him recently, mainly owing to deliberate avoidance. On the odd occasion when they had met, she had ignored him, something he had seemed happy to echo. Neither of them had wanted another conversation like the last. Instinctively she had taken care to avoid the bars during the day, and somehow she knew those would be the best places to find him. He was a day drinker. She only hoped to catch him while he was still relatively sober. This was not a discussion that would go well drunk.

She eventually found him in the upstairs bar after breakfast.

He had his back to the door, so Tara was able to approach him unnoticed until the moment she passed him to take a seat at his table. Reese glanced up from his pint of beer, shocked, then his eyebrows dropped as he narrowed his eyes at her.

"What do you want?"

Tara looked back at him steadily. It wasn't the best start to things, but had been considerably more polite than she had expected.

"I have something to say to you."

Reese eyed her suspiciously. The words *stone cold bitch* flickered in Tara's memory, and she forced her face to remain impassive.

"Like what?"

Tara took a steadying breath. "I wanted to apologize."

Whatever Reese had been expecting her to say, it clearly hadn't been that. He stared at her, jaw sagging, one hand frozen in the air halfway to his pint.

"I— Wow."

Well, it was better than nothing. He could have thrown it back in her face. Hell, he could have thrown his *drink* in her face, although he would probably have seen that as a waste of good beer.

And she would have had to slap him for that. There were limits, after all.

He was still wide-eyed and speechless, so Tara decided to elaborate.

"I didn't mean to...hurt you. I thought you just wanted sex. That's how it's always been for me."

"It's not that way for everyone," Reese cut in.

"I know. I didn't handle it very well." Tara held his gaze. She would *not* hang her head. "I should have thought about how you might feel."

"Yeah. You should." The words were blunt, but Reese's face had softened a little, and Tara thought she could see friendliness in his eyes.

Just a little.

"I honestly didn't mean to be a bitch." The memory of Azure's angry words that day on the deck flickered in her mind, and Tara let out a sigh. "I guess I've been one for a long time."

It was easier to admit than she had thought.

When she was only home briefly between deployments, it was simple to hook up with men in bars and leave immediately afterwards. Nobody got hurt, nobody had ever complained. She hadn't considered how it would work in a closed space like a yacht out in the middle of the ocean.

She hadn't considered anything at all. She had seen Reese as little more than a cock on legs. And as for everyone else—*Christ.* She could have destroyed any chance of a relationship with Azure, ruined herself in Liam's eyes and broken Ryan's heart.

She had never been so happy to have all her plans turned upside down.

The thought must have shown in her face. "Okay. I guess I can forgive you." Reese's voice was considerably warmer than before. "Just don't tell Hyde. He might kick the shit out of me."

Tara let out a startled giggle.

"Oh, hardly!"

Reese shook his head. "I'm not kidding. If I'd known he was after you I'd have stayed well away. He's bigger than me."

Tara was briefly tempted to tell him how right he was, but decided to keep that piece of information to herself.

"I think you're safe. I can keep him in line."

Reese's response was cut off by the approach of the barman, who had noticed Tara's lack of a drink. Mindful of her pain relief medication, Tara ordered a mocktail. It came bedecked with umbrellas, cherries and slices of lime, allowing very little room to actually drink it.

"So," Reese said, watching her attempt to negotiate the fruit, "is it serious between you two?"

"I— Ow." Tara removed the parasol that had poked her in the eye. Losing patience, she dumped all the garnish on the tray. "Yeah, it is."

"New for you?"

"Kind of."

"Good."

Tara arched an eyebrow at him over the rim of her glass. "Good?"

"Yeah." Reese's mouth was twisted in an undeniable smirk. "I think it's about time you met your match in someone."

The best response Tara could think of to that was a laugh. She couldn't help thinking that if she had met her match in Ryan, he sure as hell had met his match in her.

And they could play together whenever they liked.

* * * *

As she descended the steps to the main deck, she spotted a blonde figure leaning over the rail. Between the cloud of her hair whipping in the wind and the swirling fabric of her blue sundress, she was barely recognizable as Kiki.

Tara hadn't seen her the night before. She had assumed that she knew why. But the figure ahead was staring seaward, an air of melancholy hanging over her.

"Kiki?"

Kiki started, turning to face her. "Tara."

An uncomfortable silence fell, filled only by the slap of waves against the yacht.

"Well, at least we know we agree on something," Tara said finally.

"What?"

"Our opinions of Tracey."

Kiki paused, watching her, then looked away. "So you know."

"I think I was one of the last to know."

"No offense. I didn't tell anyone." Kiki let out her breath in a rush, resting her elbows on the rail. "Anyway, you're not the last. *She* doesn't know."

"Yet."

"Forget 'yet'. She's not going to know." A sharp note entered Kiki's voice. "The bitch is already making things difficult. Do you have any idea how hard it would be if she claimed adultery? She'd fleece him for every penny."

Tara blinked.

"She is pregnant, remember. He has to support her."

"Oh, fuck that!" Kiki spat. "He doesn't even love her! How is it his fault she missed a pill?"

Oh, that was just too much.

"She didn't get herself pregnant, Kiki!"

Kiki shook her head stubbornly. "She seduced him. You know how men are. If it's there, they'll take it."

Jesus. Tara forced back all the retorts springing to her tongue. Apparently Kiki saw no irony in treating Nik's wife as the mistress in their relationship. Nor did she consider that Nik might have considered *her* to be 'there' for the taking.

She's more far gone than I thought. She's fucking delusional.

As she looked at Kiki, wondering what she could say that would even be heard, she realized that on this, at least, she had been wrong. She had thought that she was no better than Kiki for what she had been doing.

But in this, Kiki was far, far worse.

Remonstrating with her would be pointless. Instead she asked the question she thought that Kiki would prefer.

"So are you two going to be together now?"

A slight smile appeared on Kiki's face.

"I think so. I mean, it's not clear yet. He has to sort all this out with Tracey first. But he's making her leave the boat, so then I'll move into his room." Another thought seemed to strike her and her eyes lit up. "So you and Ryan can have it whenever you like."

"Thank you," Tara said, for want of anything better to say.

Kiki turned back toward the sea. "Yeah, so we're a bit in limbo at the moment. But it won't be long. He just needs some time."

Tara rolled her eyes. *If you believe that, I've got some swamp land for sale.* Nik might well be fond of Kiki, but she doubted that he would have left his wife for her. Given the choice, he would have chosen Tracey. It was only by luck that Kiki was in this position.

Although, she noted, as a niggling pain in her shoulder asserted itself, it was only luck from Kiki's perspective. Nobody else had come out of this unscathed.

"What's his plan for the rest of the cruise, anyway? Is he calling it off now?"

She had been wondering about it over the last few days. The whole point of the cruise had been for Nik and Tracey to host their friends and associates. Since the hostess was being unceremoniously removed and several of the guests were in turmoil, it seemed pointless to carry on sailing. It was unlikely that Azure and Liam would be staying, and without them she would probably have worn out her welcome.

Besides, Nik would hardly be a good host in these circumstances.

"I don't know yet." Kiki shook her head. "It's all up in the air right now. It was supposed to end in Greece anyway, so..."

She shrugged, and Tara nodded. They weren't far from Greece. It would be simple to let people off there if they chose—just a matter of organising flights.

Then... What?

What would Ryan do?

Kiki was still staring out to sea, so Tara joined her at the rail, forcing down a sudden rush of panic. What *would* Ryan do? Ask her to go back to the US with him? Could she do that? Would he offer to give up his job to join her in the UK? Could she ask that of him?

Or would it all end when the cruise hit Greece?

She bit her lip, pushing her emotions further down. She didn't want to think about that yet.

But after all this time, after everything, she didn't want it to end yet. For the first time she knew herself to be truly in love. She couldn't just leave it behind.

Just get to Greece. You can worry about it there.

She let out a heavy sigh, which drew Kiki's attention.

"What's up?"

"Oh, nothing. Just thinking."

"About Ryan?"

Ugh. Kiki was too damn perceptive sometimes. Tara ignored the question, but Kiki pushed on.

"Do you think you'll see him again after you leave?"

Tara shrugged.

"You do live in England. Hmm. And you travel a lot, don't you?"

"Mmm."

Kiki paused thoughtfully for a moment then seemed to shrug it off. "Meh. I never liked him anyway."

Oh, thanks. Tara took that as her cue to leave. Kiki seemed happy enough just watching the waves—she took Tara's "Bye" with nothing more than a smile.

A long-distance relationship combined with her job in the Army. She shook her head. Yeah, that sounded like a match made in heaven.

Chapter Twenty-One

The clouds had cleared, and beams of light glistened on the veil of glass that separated them. Slipping a second dry biscuit into her mouth, Azure rested one hand on the window frame, her gaze intent on the lone figure out on the deck.

She was alone herself. Liam had gone down to the kitchens a few minutes earlier. He had taken to managing her cravings like a duck to water. By the time they got home he would have a full list of instructions for their cook, as well as probably a whole team of obstetricians on call.

They were to leave in the next few days.

"I know how you feel," Liam had said. "I don't like cutting vacations short either. But I won't have that happening again. I just won't."

"I know. It scared me too."

Liam had wrapped her in his arms, cradling her head in the crook of his shoulder. "I just want you safe."

Azure could understand. And in any event, she had no real need to stay on board. For her, the trip had fulfilled its purpose.

Leaning back on the rail as she was, the lines of Tara's body were softened, at rest. With her head tilted back, her sunglasses mirroring sunlight, she looked peaceful, as if her eyes were focused on nothing.

It was an image Azure wanted to remember forever.

As Tara turned to face the view, pushing the shades upwards to rest on her head, Azure opened the door and stepped out to meet her.

It was a bright day, a golden day.

Idly dangling her wrists in the air, Tara let the sun beat down on her skin and watched the Zakynthian coastline bob in the distance.

She had heard good things about Zakynthos. There was a cove with a shipwrecked boat somewhere, apparently. Izzie had been there once with a Club 18–30 group and had raved about the fantastic bars and nightclubs. She had always called the island Zante, but Tara had since learned that both names were correct.

There was nothing to be done, no plan ahead. A day of relaxation. No need to deal with Tracey and the wreck of her marriage, no need to listen to Kiki and the possible resurrection of her plans with Nik... No need to deal with anything.

Just relax, alone with the Greek sun... And Ryan.

If he ever got out of bed, of course.

Tara let a smile cross her face at the image of a tanned, blond — *truly* blond — Ryan tangled in the sheets, and found that it remained in place even as the sound of footsteps told her that Azure was about to join her at the rail.

Her automatic greeting was pre-empted by Azure's.

"You have freshly-fucked hair."

"I beg your pardon? I do *not*." Tara punched a snickering Azure in the shoulder. "Shut up."

Without answering, Azure fixed her with a long, knowing look, before turning back to the view. Tara resisted the urge to smooth her hair.

"So where is the blond Adonis anyway?"

"Still in bed. And no earthy remarks from you."

"No, no." Azure held up a conciliatory hand. "Not at all. I'm sure he's…had a hard night."

"Watch it. I could still push you over the side."

"Give it a couple of months." Azure glanced down ruefully at her stomach. "I'll be suitably whale-like by then."

Tara resisted the temptation to say something scathing. Azure looked exactly as she always did—soft and curvaceous. Even dressed as she was in a crimson sundress clearly chosen for maternity, there was nothing to show her pregnancy, and when the breeze pressed the cotton against her stomach there was no sign of a fecund swell.

Still, there was a glow to her skin that rivalled the sunlight, and an air of ease—of security—that Tara knew only half came from within.

The thought gave way to a question.

"Where's Liam?"

Azure smiled.

"Down in the kitchen. I told him I was craving lime cheesecake, so he's gone to make sure they've got some for lunch."

"You've got him well tr—" Tara began automatically, then stopped.

Azure cast her a sideways look, but said nothing. Tara bit her lip.

You're being unfair. It's a nice thing to do. You'd want someone to do that for you.

Except that she would probably have done it herself.

But it wasn't the cheesecake.

It was the reminder of everything else—the continual cocoon, the engulfing in softness, and the way that Azure seemed to accept sleeping on feathers and living force-shielded with Liam as a perpetual barrier to every potential hazard.

It was a picture she could never see herself in. For a moment she imagined Ryan hanging about her, wrapping around her like a coiled snake, and felt her face twist as if tasting bile, fingers automatically twitching.

I'd go mad.

Azure was still looking at her, that expectant expression on her face, and Tara finally spoke.

"How can you take it? He'd stifle me."

After a pause, Azure nodded, turning back to look at the sea. It was a moment before she answered.

"He won't let me fall."

In the silence that followed, the sound of waves breaking made itself heard as the coastline ahead drew nearer.

"Anyway," Azure said, a mocking note in her voice, "I couldn't live with your blond piece of ass. He'd drive me up the pole."

"That better not be another innuendo. And the word is arse."

Azure laughed, bumping Tara with her shoulder.

"A few months with Ryan and it'll be 'ass'—he talks about yours all the time, like what a hot little—"

"Oh, shut up!"

Tara pushed her, dodged out of the way of Azure's return shove, then they were both batting at each other, giggling stupidly. For a few moments, they were kids again.

A wave hit, and the deck rolled. Without thinking, Tara caught Azure's shoulders and steadied her. Azure looked up at her, a slight smirk crossing her face.

"I wouldn't have fallen."

Tara narrowed her eyes for a second, considering several rude responses, before settling for a martyrish shake of the head.

Okay, so maybe Azure was just the type of person who attracted protection. These days, anyway. And especially now she was pregnant. She had only confided the news a few days prior, it apparently being past the most dangerous time.

"Are you sure it'll be okay?" Tara had asked.

"As much as I can be." Azure had given a casual shrug. "The risk period is the first three months, and all mine were in that time."

Tara had nodded slowly. That sounded hopeful. And certainly Liam would have organized the best medical care possible. The thought had led to another question.

"Are you going to find out the sex?"

"Oh yeah." A wicked grin had crossed Azure's face. "Liam's hoping it's twins."

"Christ. No pressure then."

"I'll see what I can manage." Azure had rested a hand on her stomach for a moment, gazing down at it with an expression that had sent a warm feeling to Tara's heart.

"Do you want a boy or a girl?"

"Either. We've picked out names for both." Azure had flicked a finger at her bookshelf, where *The Big Book of Baby Names* stood prominently. "William James for a boy, Natalie Julia for a girl. If it's twins, God help us. "

"You always said you wanted a huge family."

"I might change my mind after this pops out."

"They don't 'pop out', dear."

"Yeah, that's what I'm worried about. Friend back home had one a few months ago. She said it was like getting an orange through a hosepipe."

Tara had shaken her head, laughing, as Azure had pulled a 'freaked-out' face before looking down at her non-existent bump again.

It was so good to see.

I really hope this works out.

"I called Mum," Azure had added, looking back up. "I think she'll come down off the ceiling in a couple of days."

Tara had laughed. "Sounds about right."

"Yup. Dad's doing his stiff upper lip thing, but I think he's pleased." Azure had held up her mobile phone. "News is spreading. I got calls from Izzie and Roger earlier. At least I think it was Izzie. I couldn't tell for all the screaming."

That sounded exactly like Izzie, and Tara couldn't help thinking that excited screaming might be a better strategy than nerves, which had hit her immediately. Despite Azure's outward calm, Tara had found herself on edge ever since.

In the end, unable to conceal her worry, she had been forced to tell Ryan about her own miscarriage. Ryan had responded better than she had expected. He had wrapped her up in his arms, held her, and told her over and over that it was going to be all right.

Somehow, after half an hour of this, Tara had found herself almost believing him.

Despite this, Ryan had had a hell of a time convincing her to calm down and stop stressing herself out. He had eventually resorted to fucking her against a wall, which struck Tara as more of an incentive to repeat the behavior than anything else, but she had chosen not to tell him that.

As if reading her mind, Ryan appeared behind her.

"Hey, Golden Girl."

"Hey." Tara smiled up at him. Taking care to avoid her shoulder, Ryan hooked an arm around her and gently pulled her flush against his chest.

After Azure had told her of her and Liam's ultimate plans, she had mentioned them to Ryan, wanting to test the waters. His response had been remarkably calm.

"That might be a good idea, actually. For you, I mean."

"For me?" The words had come out angrily, but in Tara's head her immediate thought had been *Just me?* That sounded as though Ryan was planning to stay on board without her.

Ryan had held up a hand at the outrage in her voice. "No, I'm not trying to get rid of you. I'm thinking about your shoulder."

"It's fine," Tara had said automatically, even as she'd rotated her shoulder experimentally and winced.

"You need to be near decent medical care. A physio, at least."

Tara had sighed, acknowledging the truth. She had already undergone some physiotherapy, which had been enough to show her just how long her recovery was likely to be. Her shoulder was stiff and uncooperative. She knew the military hospital would be able to help, but everything would have to be on hold for a while.

She hadn't told her parents yet. It was Azure's time to shine. In any case, her mother would worry about her health and her father about her career. He was already dissatisfied with her progress up the ranks— God knows how he would feel about her taking sick leave over what he would view as a minor injury.

She definitely needed proper medical treatment, and while the on-board doctor was good at his job, he couldn't provide everything.

Nik had made it clear that everyone on board was welcome to remain until the end of the cruise, which had been originally scheduled to visit several Greek islands before ending on Kos. However, Zakynthos was a convenient place to leave, and she knew that Ryan was right.

But she didn't want to go yet.

"I know I do. I just—" She'd broken off, unable to formulate her thoughts into words. This was a part of being in love that she *hated*. She despised herself for feeling so needy, so vulnerable.

So *scared*.

"Don't worry." Ryan had cocked his head in mock sympathy. "I'll hold your hand on the plane."

Tara had blinked.

"You'd leave with me?"

"Of course I would, dumb-ass. Who else is going to take care of you?"

"But you live in America."

"I'm still on vacation. And Nik has offices in the UK I can work from in the short term." Ryan had smirked at the look of shock on her face. "So don't worry, we can figure it out."

Oh, thank God.

"Okay."

She had done her best to sound casual, but from the slightly smug look in Ryan's eyes, he hadn't been fooled in the least.

So it had all been decided. They would fly out from Zakynthos in three days' time, along with the Wilders, who would be flying back to the US—as was Tracey Sugiyama.

Tracey had left the boat a few days previously. As Tara understood it, she was staying in a hotel for the moment—at Nik's expense. Kiki had shortly afterwards moved all her belongings into Nik's cabin, which left Tara with a free room whenever she and Ryan needed it.

Which was where she had left him this morning. It had been a hell of a night.

"Got some news," Ryan said, drawing her attention back to the present. "Nik's divorce isn't going to go as smoothly as he'd hoped."

"Oh? Why?" *Smoothly?* To Tara's mind, there was nothing smooth about negotiating child support payments, housing and wage garnishment with the ex-wife of a billionaire.

"I just spoke to Kiki. Tracey found out about them and now she's claiming adultery. She's spent the last couple of days lining up all the best lawyers."

"What? How the hell did that happen?"

"He had naked photos of Kiki on his phone."

Speechless, Tara could only shake her head. It was just one more thing to wonder over. She couldn't help thinking that, even though she didn't especially care for Tracey, things were on their way toward being set right. Nik had cheated, after all. He could hardly claim the moral high ground, regardless of what Tracey had done.

God only knew how Kiki would be taking the news. With loud complaints to all and sundry, she imagined. Somehow she wasn't convinced that any relationship between her and Nik would last in the wake of a hellish and public divorce, but she was very glad that it wasn't her problem.

"Kiki's going nuts," Ryan added, confirming her thoughts.

"I bet."

"Yeah. Why did he leave his phone where she could find it? Why didn't he delete the photos? Why can't the stupid bitch just leave us alone? You know the type of thing."

Tara did. Somehow she thought that Kiki and Nik might just be made for each other.

She heard footsteps approaching from her left. Turning, she saw Liam join Azure at the rail. Wrapping an arm around her, he whispered something in her ear, letting his hand rest on her stomach at the same time. Azure smiled and answered, leaning back into his embrace.

They look perfect together.

The image reminded Tara of something. Ryan had just turned to speak to Azure. After glancing round to make sure that nobody was watching, she slid a hand into her back pocket and drew out a small photograph. For a moment she held it against her chest, concealing it with her hand.

It was her treasured photo of Liam.

After arriving back on the ship, she had spent a long time holding the photo, mulling over what had happened.

So much had taken place since she had first met Liam. So much had changed. He was no longer the perfect individual in the shot, no longer the jerk-off fantasy she had dreamt of.

He was just a man.

Azure's man.

And she no longer had any need of the photo. It was only sentimentality that kept it with her.

Now, she looked again at the photo and smiled.

Slightly bent at the corners, a little faded around the edges, but still something she had kept for years, prized, and now… Now something she was glad not to need anymore.

Ryan was still speaking to Azure. With one more quick look round, Tara leaned farther forward, dangled her hand over the rail and let go, watching as the delicate square of color fluttered away on the breeze.

A song she had listened to so often echoed in her head, and Tara smiled as two of the lines now took on new meaning.

I don't want your photograph…

I don't need your photograph…

It was over, and she now had Azure and Liam, and more importantly Ryan. And that was all that mattered.

Epilogue

One year later

"Ryan, did you pick up the tickets?"

"Relax. They're in my jacket."

"I am relaxed. I just don't want to get there and find we've forgotten something."

Ryan popped his blond head out of their bedroom door. "You've planned this trip like a commando mission. There is no way in hell we've forgotten anything."

Tara shook her head, laughing. Despite herself, she had to admit that Ryan was right. They had been preparing for their trip to the US for weeks. She had everything scheduled down to the second.

It was strange to think that just over a year ago she had been dreading seeing her sister and Liam again.

She had moved in with Ryan six months earlier.

Initially, on returning from the cruise, she had stayed at her parents' house on the base for easy access to the military hospital. However, her father's attitude had soon made the situation intolerable. He had harangued her continually about the time it was taking for her to recover.

"Dad, you know perfectly well how gunshot wounds work."

Her father had shaken his head. "When I was injured in the line of duty, I didn't waste my time lazing around, young lady. I—"

Tara had cut him off, "I am not lazing around, and I'll be following the physio's advice, not yours. Drop it."

Her father's next point of attack had been the presence of the bullet in her shoulder, which he'd insisted was impeding her recovery. To shut him up, Tara had agreed to an operation to remove it—which had proven to be a bad idea. A hospital infection had left her bedridden for a month.

Shortly afterwards she had packed her bags and moved out.

Ryan, in the meantime, had been renting a flat in town. Tara had originally planned to move into a hotel, but had been spurred on to move in with Ryan after the final argument with her father, who hadn't been enamored of her boyfriend at all. This was partially because he was American, but primarily because, as Tara had discovered afterwards, during her illness Ryan had torn a strip off him in the hospital corridor.

She was beginning to see why Azure had felt the need to rebel against their father. Until then she had always followed his decrees, but now… Now he was being a jerk, frankly. He had seen plenty of gunshot wounds during his time in the military. He knew perfectly well that recovery took as long as it took. If he was going to harass her about it, then he could go and boil his head.

Moving in with Ryan had been easier than she had expected. She had never even considered living with a man before. The thought of constant arguments over housework, cooking, the remote control... Ugh. But somehow they had managed to find their way around every issue, and Tara had to admit that living together was a much better arrangement than she had anticipated.

It wasn't a large flat. The kitchen opened into the living room, allowing space for a small dining table as well as two plushy sofas and a wide flat-screen television. The décor was reasonably modern, if a little mismatched, torn as it was between Ryan's framed photographs of seascapes and Tara's military memorabilia. And there was only one bedroom, which meant that any arguments had to be resolved before nightfall or risk someone sleeping on the couch.

But somehow they had never had difficulty on that score. Admittedly angry sex was probably not the recommended method for hashing out disagreements, but it seemed to work well enough.

Ryan had been a great help during her recovery. He was especially good at dispelling her frustrations at the time it was taking. And it was frustrating. She had hoped to be up to speed within a few months, and instead it had taken a year. Still, it was amazing how easily problems disappeared with just a well-placed application of Ryan's tongue.

But she was still on sick leave, which at least meant that this trip had been straightforward to arrange. She had been wanting to visit Azure ever since the birth.

"You've got to come over," Azure had told her on the phone. "They're dying to meet their aunt."

"Oh, come on. They're two weeks old."

"Oh, all right. *I'm* dying for them to meet their aunt." Tara had almost been able to hear Azure rolling her eyes.

"You just want me to help you out on night shifts, I bet."

Azure had laughed. "Well, if anyone has experience with twins, it's us."

Liam's hope for twins had come to fruition. Tara supposed it was only to be expected. Sometimes twins ran in families, after all. When Azure had emailed Tara the ultrasound that showed two foetuses, she had sounded thrilled—though the excitement had dimmed a little as the months had passed and Azure had gradually become spectacularly, uncomfortably huge.

The final email before the birth had been one extremely direct line.

I just want them OUT!

Whether she had felt the same way during the hours of labor Tara didn't know, but from the report she had had from Liam, all had gone well. The babies were healthy, Azure had recovered nicely, and dozens of photographs had been emailed over—Natalie Julia sleeping, Anoushka Marie wearing one of the little caps Tara had sent, staring at the camera with a look of utter bemusement.

From being a woman who had at one time kept only one photograph, Tara had begun keeping albums full of them. Her Facebook was full of baby pictures. And she kept one on the mantelpiece, there to be looked at and cooed over every time she passed it.

She was unashamed about adoring her nieces. And it was far healthier to gaze at a photograph of them than it had been to obsess over a shot of their father. Far healthier.

To Tara's surprise, Azure hadn't hired a nanny — although that was probably unfair. There was no real reason for her to hire one, other than the simple fact that she could afford it. The daily photos showed Azure and Liam — who had given himself the full two weeks of paternity leave — taking the girls out every day, around the gardens or the quieter areas of the park, and if they were accompanied by bodyguards, the shots were carefully framed to conceal that fact.

It was a necessary part of their life, but Tara couldn't help thinking that it wasn't right. The thought of her sister and nieces in danger made her rage. Being attacked in public may have been part of *her* life, but she was damned if she would accept it as part of Azure's.

"Okay," Ryan said as he came out of the bedroom, bringing Tara back to the present. "We're all set." He picked up the photograph from the mantelpiece and handed it to her. "Don't forget this."

Tara took the photo and glanced at it, a smile crossing her face. Two small faces looked back at her, with identical tufts of dark hair, identical green eyes and identical baby smiles. One was dressed in a green onesie, the other in purple.

"Which is which again?" Ryan asked, looking at the photo over her shoulder.

"Natalie is in green, Anoushka in purple."

Ryan shook his head. "I'll never tell them apart. They should have been like you two. No chance of mixing up blonde and black." He disappeared back into the bedroom, leaving Tara smiling thoughtfully.

She knew what Ryan had meant. She and Azure, while similar facially, could never have been mistaken for each other. But another, sadder image had come to mind — twin sisters who had had what had seemed to be an irreparable rift, born of hidden hurt and refusal to communicate.

God, I hope Anoushka and Natalie are never like us.

She could have missed out on all of this. If she had declined that invitation, had pushed harder to seduce Liam, she could have been still stuck in her old life, with an intact shoulder and a stone cold heart.

At least now she could face the prospect of staying in Liam Wilder's mansion with a calm perspective. In the past it would have sent her into a tailspin. Now it was simply a convenient way to avoid the expense of a hotel and to see her sister and nieces every day. They would be installed in the guest wing, which according to Azure was big enough to be a house in its own right, and they could be completely independent if they so desired — the staff were happy to prepare food for them separately. Apparently after dealing with Azure's cravings for stuffed jalapeño peppers and deep-fried ice cream at midnight they were able to cope with just about anything.

Tara had seen photos of the mansion, as well as some of their bedroom. It had a view of the gardens, an en suite bathroom and a curtained four-poster bed that intrigued Ryan. Fortunately they were far enough away from the master wing that they could be assured of complete privacy should they feel the urge to christen the room — or the bath, the shower or the balcony. That said, Tara remembered Azure's tale of tearing the curtains off her bed and hoped to goodness that they wouldn't end up doing that themselves. That would be awkward to explain.

Occasionally she wondered if Azure had told Liam about their liaison. It had never been mentioned since the cruise. Tara hoped that it would remain that way. It only flickered into her head at times when conversations about the twins reminded her of her miscarriage.

Thinking about it now, she felt the smile drop from her face. It was an old memory and no longer treasured as a link to Liam, but still she felt her insides stir painfully at the thought. The time spent at home resting, her career on hold, had made her wonder about having children.

Maybe her biological clock was ticking.

She shook her head, forcing the thought back, and tucked the photo into her pocket. It wouldn't be long before they had to leave for the airport.

California. God, that was going to be a long flight. At least thirteen hours. It was a good-sized plane, so there should be decent space and food—in airplane terms, at least—but she had never enjoyed long-haul flights. In fact, she had never liked flying at all. She hated all the preparation, the waiting around in the airport, the constant checks and queuing. Not to mention having to deal with connecting flights. It was such a pain. And, much to her annoyance, she always felt sick after getting off a plane. It was a standing joke in the family that, after flying, she was so ill she looked exactly like her passport photo.

She crossed the room to the sofa, where their two carry-on bags were lying, and unzipped hers, meaning to check what she had packed. She knew there would be in-flight movies, but still, the flight would be interminable without decent reading material.

She dug around for a moment, confused when she didn't find her Kindle. *I'm sure I put it in here—oh, wait.* An Andy McNab novel half buried in a polo shirt looked up at her. This was Ryan's bag.

I'm seriously losing it.

She was just about to withdraw her hand when her fingers closed around something hard.

Something small and box-shaped.

She took it out and looked at it. It was a small jeweler's box, the kind used for earrings – or a ring.

A ring.

She listened for a moment. Ryan was still moving around in the bedroom. Quickly she opened the box, immediately drawn to the glistening jewel inside.

It was a princess-cut diamond ring on a platinum band.

He's going to ask me to marry him.

Her first reaction was to stare in awe at the ring. It was exactly what she would have chosen for herself. Azure's engagement ring had been a large heart-cut solitaire on rose gold – beautiful, but, to Tara's taste, a little excessive. She didn't much care for gold of any color and found most fancy cuts to be too fussy. Not to mention diamond clusters. They were like slapping someone in the face with a roll of bills.

But this! It was stunning. She could already picture it on her finger. Simple lines, no gold, and not ostentatiously large.

Still, the meaning of it made it suddenly seem much larger.

She forced her way through the conflicting thoughts crashing around in her head. It might just be a gift. He might not be planning to propose to her.

But then he might.

Am I ready for this?

She had never been a person to plan her own wedding, or to even picture herself getting married. These last months with Ryan had been the first that she had spent in a proper live-in relationship. Could she see herself marrying him?

And if she did, what would it mean for her? Would it just be a matter of continuing as they were, with the name of Tara Hyde instead of Tara Thornton? Would Ryan even expect her to change her name? She had never given it any real thought, but it didn't strike her as something to argue about. Her friends had sometimes debated 'taking a man's name', but hell, Thornton was her father's name. She could take it or leave it.

What about his career? Or hers? Ryan had been working in the company's UK offices, but Tara had never expected that to be a permanent arrangement. At some point Ryan would probably want to move back to the US—which would mean her moving with him. Could she really do that? Give up her own career for his?

But then, thinking about it, she wouldn't be. Not really.

She had been on sick leave now for a year. The thought of going back out on deployment no longer appealed. She could still have a career in the US without the constant tours of duty.

And, she realized, she would be happy to do that. Happy to move to America for him.

Happy, in fact, to marry him.

The sound of footsteps in the bedroom brought her back to her senses. Swiftly she shoved the box back into Ryan's bag and picked up her own just as Ryan appeared in the living room, dragging their wheeled cases behind him.

"Okay. Suitcases are locked. We're good to go."

Tara turned to face him. "Great. Let's go then."

Ryan threw her a grin. "Sure you're ready?"

She knew what he meant, but Tara remembered the engagement ring and smiled back. "Hell yeah, I'm ready."

And with that, her new life was waiting.

About the Author

I have been writing for ten years and first got into erotic romance through the Romantic Novelists' Association New Writer's Scheme; they critiqued my debut novel 'The Hand He Dealt', which was published in June 2011 and was nominated for the Joan Hessayon Award.

I live in Yorkshire with my husband and two extremely bratty tuxedo cats. When I'm not writing I spend my time watching horror movies, listening to rock music, travelling to new places and trying out new restaurants.

Tanith Davenport loves to hear from readers. You can find her contact information, website details and author profile page at http://www.totallybound.com.

Totally Bound Publishing

Home of Erotic Romance

Lightning Source UK Ltd.
Milton Keynes UK
UKOW03f1510120514
231547UK00001B/9/P